Love can heal even the worst of wounds.

Hansen has spent the past few years saving people. He likes his life, but there's one thing missing — his mate. He yearns for that kind of connection, even though there's nothing he can do to find the one person who's destined to be his.

Evan has spent the past few years in a cage. The last thing he expected when he was taken out of it and used as leverage by a hunter was to find his long-lost best friend — and his mate. After everything he went through and the fact that he's now a mutant, he's not sure what he's ready for, but he won't let the hunters and the doctors win.

Hansen and Evan find their way to each other, but their fight won't be over until all the labs are closed and the hunters are gone. The problem is that no one knows how to make that happen or how long it will take.

Or what will happen to the mutants and their loved ones in the meantime.

Hansen
Copyright © 2025 Catherine Lievens
ISBN: 978-1-4874-4326-9
Cover art by Martine Jardin

Published by Extasy Books Inc

Look for us online at:
www.extasybooks.com

HANSEN

MUTANTS SERIES BOOK 7

BY

CATHERINE LIEVENS

CHAPTER ONE

Evan didn't want to do this. He *really* didn't want to do this.

He'd been hurt enough in his life not to want to do the same to someone else. He wasn't sure what was happening, but there weren't a thousand reasons for a hunter to take him out of his cage and sneak him out while trying not to get anyone's attention.

Evan was used to dealing with hunters. He had no idea how long he'd been a prisoner, but it had to have been years by now. He'd been moved from facility to facility, punched and beaten, laughed at and insulted. Nothing good ever came from hunters, and this one wouldn't be any different.

For a moment after the hunter had taken Evan out of his cage, Evan had thought he was about to die. He was still torn about how he felt about that. Part of him just wanted all of

1

this to be over, but another part didn't want to give the hunters and the doctors the satisfaction of killing him. Evan was stronger than people thought — stronger than he thought sometimes. *That* was why he was still alive. It was why he was finally out of his cage.

He didn't know the reason why the hunter had taken him out, though. He'd stuffed Evan into a small box in the back of his van, and they'd driven for a while. If Evan had to choose, he'd pick a cage instead of a box. It was roomier and let in more light.

He'd snickered as he stumbled out of the box, and the hunter had stared at him like he was losing his mind. He felt it was better for him to laugh than to cry, even though it made him feel like he was nuts. It was probably a sign of how traumatized he was that he could see humor in all of this. What was he going to do, anyway? Scream for help? No one ever came, and he'd stopped doing that a long time ago.

Which was how he'd ended up standing in an alley. He looked around, then back at the hunter. "You want me to do *what*?"

The hunter glared. He smelled bad, but when Evan tried moving away, he tightened his hold on Evan's arm and shook him.

"You heard me. You're going to go to the door and knock and come up with an excuse to get Orion to step out of the bakery."

"Are you going to hurt him?" It was obvious, but Evan needed to waste time. Maybe someone would walk by and notice them. Maybe they'd stop Evan before he could help the hunter hurt this Orion guy.

"None of your business." The hunter reached behind himself and pulled out a gun from the waistband of his dirty jeans. "You better obey. You won't like what happens if you don't."

Evan was tempted to tell him that nothing he could do with that gun could be worse than what had already been done to him in the labs, but he didn't want to push it. Maybe it wouldn't be a bad thing if the hunter shot him. He would never have to go back to the lab. He could finally rest.

"I won't help you hurt him," Evan said with more conviction than he felt.

He should have known better than to stand up to a hunter. The man didn't shoot him. Instead, he raised his gun and hit Evan on the side of the face, right where Evan was already bruised. Pain exploded under Evan's skin, and he stumbled back, reaching out to hold himself up against the wall. The alley wasn't particularly dirty, but his stomach heaved anyway.

Of course, it wasn't like he was clean. He couldn't remember the last time he had a shower. The doctors in the lab kept him clean when they needed to poke at him, but beyond that, they didn't care, and the hunters cared even less. Evan supposed it was hypocritical of him to judge the hunter for his stench when he probably smelled just as bad, but at least the hunter had access to a shower. Evan didn't.

"You're going to do what I tell you to do," the hunter said through gritted teeth. His gaze flickered to the back door of the bakery. "I'll kill you if you don't."

"Then kill me." Pain pulsed in Evan's face. He wasn't sure he was bleeding, but he wouldn't be surprised if he was. He reached up to clean whatever seeped there with the sleeve of his oversized hoodie. It was black, so it wouldn't stain any more than it already was.

The hunter smiled. He was missing several teeth, and his breath smelled of beer and decay. Evan heaved, but he managed not to throw up, probably because he couldn't remember the last time he'd eaten something.

"I'll kill you, then I'll kill my son. Or maybe I'll do it the other way around so you can see what happens when someone disobeys my orders."

This Orion guy was the hunter's son? Hunters really were monsters, weren't they? "If you're going to kill him anyway, you can get him out of the bakery without me."

The hunter raised his gun again, but he didn't hit Evan this time. He ran the muzzle of the gun down Evan's cheek, then tapped it on Evan's lower lip. "So you want to die."

"Wouldn't you?"

"There are worse things that I can do to you than kill you. Do you want to find out what those things are?"

Evan didn't even want to *think* about them. He thought he'd stopped feeling fear a long time ago, but he was starting to realize that wasn't the case. He was terrified at the thought of what this man could do. The other hunters and the doctors had hurt him, but they'd never violated him. Something told Evan that was what this man was suggesting.

He couldn't. If something like that happened to him, he'd fracture, and he wouldn't be able to pull himself back together ever again.

He breathed out. "Fine. I'll go."

The hunter nodded. "Knock on the door and get him to step out in the alley."

Evan hated himself for doing this, but he didn't have an alternative. He'd hoped the hunter would kill him if he said no, but that wasn't going to happen, and he couldn't deal with anything else.

He moved closer to the door. He glanced back, and the hunter narrowed his eyes at him. There was a silent threat in his eyes that Evan couldn't ignore, so he quickly knocked before pulling the hood of his hoodie up. Whoever opened the door would be alarmed if they saw the state his face was in.

The door opened to reveal a big man. Evan sucked in a breath and quickly took a step back, even though he didn't think the man would hurt him. Why would he? He didn't know him. He was big, though, with blond hair and muscles that made him look like he could break Evan in half without getting out of breath. There was a streak of flour on his cheek, which looked oddly out of place on him.

"Can I help you?" the man asked.

Evan wrapped his arms around himself. He didn't know if

this was Orion, but who else could it be? "I'm really sorry about this," he said.

Evan knew the moment the man noticed the bruise on his face because he sucked in a breath. He opened the door wider so he could move closer to Evan, doing exactly what his father had expected.

"Who hurt you?" the man asked.

Evan shook his head. "I didn't want to do this. He forced me."

"Good boy," the hunter drawled, making Evan want to puke.

The shock on the baker's face was obvious. He hadn't expected the hunter to be there. He clearly didn't want anything to do with him because he moved back towards the bakery. His hands tightened into fists at his sides as if he were ready to fight the hunter.

Part of Evan hoped he would.

But before the baker — Orion, he had to be Orion — could do anything, the hunter grabbed Evan around the neck. Evan squeaked and tried to pull the arm away, but he couldn't. The hunter had a good hold on him, and he wasn't giving it up.

"You're going to come with us," the hunter said.

Orion shook his head. "I can't leave."

"Yes, you can, and you will, because otherwise, Evan will pay the price." He squeezed his arm around Evan's throat. "Won't you?"

Evan wasn't sure if the hunter was talking to him, but the answer was obvious. Of course the hunter would hurt Evan if his son refused to come along. It was why he'd taken Evan out of his cage. He'd wanted to use him, and he was.

And there was nothing Evan could do about it.

*

Hansen was jealous. He couldn't look away from Eliza and Olga. Why was he sitting with them again? Why did he have to watch them as they cuddled and smiled at each other? This was what happened when he agreed to get a drink with his friends. He'd always been a weepy drunk, and while he wasn't there yet, it wouldn't take many more drinks for him to reach that point.

"I wish I had a mate. Period," he told Davey. "It's not fair. Why is everyone finding their mate, but I'm not?" He glanced at Olga. Maybe she could help. She could see the future, so maybe she'd seen Hansen's. He didn't need to know everything, just whether or not he would meet his mate and when it would happen. He was tired of waiting, but if he knew how long it would take, he could make his peace with it. "Have you seen anything? Is my mate coming?"

"You know I can't tell you," she said as she squeezed her mate tighter against her side. They were so happy that it made Hansen want to cry.

Maybe he'd drunk a little more than he remembered.

"But I want to find my mate. Even Davey found his, and have you seen Orion? He's gorgeous."

"Don't talk about my mate like that," Davey warned. There was no heat in his voice because he knew that Hansen would never do anything to hurt their friendship. Besides, Orion only had eyes for Davey.

That was what Hansen wanted. He wanted someone who would fit into his life, someone who would make him happy and that he could make happy. He wasn't afraid of hard work when it came to relationships, but he'd stopped dating a while ago, and he missed it. He missed having something like that to look forward to and having someone to cuddle with and to talk to. He missed intimacy, holding hands, and tender kisses on the couch while watching TV.

What was the point of doing all of that with someone who wasn't his mate? He couldn't shake the feeling that it would be a betrayal, and with his luck, he'd meet his mate right after getting serious with someone. No, he didn't want that to happen, which meant that the next person he would date was his mate.

"I have eyes, Davey. What am I supposed to do when I see him? Look away? That would be kind of weird, and I'm pretty sure Orion would want to know what's up with me," he explained. He was proud that his voice wasn't slurring.

"You're so dramatic," Olga teased.

"I just want to finally start something, you know? I've been hunting scientists and liberating people for years now, and I've never had anything for myself. I want that to change."

"You could date," Davey offered.

Hansen shook his head. "Only my mate." He'd done one-night stands, dates, and even serious relationships. None of them could compare to what he could see between Olga and Eliza or between Davey and Orion. *That* was what he wanted.

He lost track of the conversation as he thought about his mate hiding somewhere out there. He was startled when Olga and Eliza got to their feet to leave. It was later than he'd realized, but he hadn't exactly been watching the clock. He wasn't ready to leave yet, so he was glad that Davey seemed okay staying with him for a bit longer. There'd been something going on with him, and while Hansen had been curious, he hadn't wanted to push. Maybe it was time to.

He hadn't expected Davey to answer his questions, but Davey did, shocking him. He shocked him even more when he told him about his best friend and what had happened to him. Hansen had been in a lab, like all of them. He knew what the scientists and the doctors did to people, and he could understand why Davey was so frantic. He wanted to get his best friend out of whatever lab he was in. No one should be stuck in one of those places. They were hell on earth.

"Have you told anyone else about this?" he asked.

"Moore and Orion."

"And what did they say?" It was clear that Davey felt guilty about what had happened, but he had no reason to. He might not listen to Hansen if he said that, but surely, he'd listen to his mate.

"You already know what they said," Davey said with a glare. "You don't have to ask."

"Well, if you believed them, you wouldn't be feeling guilty.

If Evan was your best friend, he wouldn't want you to be unhappy." The same went for Hansen. He might be unhappy because he didn't have a mate, but he would never begrudge his friends for finding theirs.

"But I'm supposed to focus on getting him back, not on building a life with my mate," Davey argued.

"Let me ask you this." Hansen turned to face Davey, tucking his leg under himself to be more comfortable. "How would you feel if your roles were reversed? If you'd been left behind while Evan was free? What would you do if, when he found you, he told you he'd met his mate and had built a life with them? Would you think he'd been wasting time instead of trying to find you, or would you be happy that he had support?"

"I'd be happy for him." Davey sighed. "I know he'd be happy for me. It's not like I can look for him twenty-four-seven. He'd understand that."

"There you go. I realize it's much harder to actually deal with this, but as long as Evan wasn't an asshole, he wouldn't want you to slowly kill yourself to find him. He certainly wouldn't want you to ignore your mate."

"I'm not."

"I know. I'm sure Evan would be happy for you, and it's not like you're going to stop trying to find him. You've been through a lot. We all have, and we're still dealing with all the consequences. Don't make yourself unhappy just because you feel like you have to be. There's no doubt what Evan's gone through is horrible, but it doesn't make what *you* went through any less awful."

Hansen squeaked when Davey unexpectedly pulled him into a hug. "Thank you," Davey murmured.

"Just don't hug me to death," Hansen said, hugging Davey back.

They didn't linger long after that. Davey was probably eager to get to his mate, and Hansen couldn't blame him. He'd want the same if he had someone like Orion waiting for him at home. Hell, he wouldn't care even if his mate was nothing like Orion. Orion was handsome and sweet, and he was exactly what Davey needed, but Hansen didn't care what his mate looked like. He didn't care about his mate's name or what they did for a living. He just wanted to meet them.

Apparently, that was too much to ask for.

"You're sure you're steady enough to go home on your own?" Davey asked as they walked out of the bar.

"I'll be fine. Go find your mate and cuddle him."

"You'll find someone eventually," Davey promised.

Hansen glared at him. "My *mate.*"

"Yes, I hope that someone will be your mate, but maybe think about the fact that not everyone meets theirs or that you could meet them in ten or twenty years. Do you really want to be alone all that time?"

Hansen didn't, but what choice did he have? He wanted to wait for his mate. He didn't expect his mate to do the same, but he didn't think he could be with someone when he knew there would be no future with them.

He was still thinking about Davey's words as he walked toward home. What would happen if he never met his mate? Would he be alone forever? Was it something he could deal with, or should he give up waiting?

He wasn't ready to do that just yet. Maybe he'd wait a few more weeks or months before surrendering. He wasn't in a hurry, even though sometimes, he was a bit lonely.

He just wished his mate would hurry up.

*

"You're going to come with us," the hunter ordered.

Orion looked like he wouldn't have any of that. Evan didn't blame him. If a hunter ordered him to do anything, he'd resist, too. Hell, he *had* resisted, which is why he was bleeding.

"Why should I come with you?" Orion asked.

"Because without me, you don't have anything. Come on. Get in the van."

Orion crossed his massive arms over his bulging chest and shook his head. "I'm not getting into that van, and I'm not going anywhere with you. Where the fuck were you when I was wounded and almost died? Perseus took care of me, just like he always does."

Evan had no idea what Orion was talking about, but it was interesting, almost like he was watching TV. God, it had been so long since he'd watched anything. He couldn't believe how many episodes of his favorite series he'd missed. And what if it had been canceled? He'd survived the labs and the hunters, but he wasn't sure he'd survive that.

"How did you get wounded? Were you helping one of these animals?" the hunter asked. He shook Evan, making his teeth rattle. If he wasn't currently stuck with the man's arm around his throat, Evan would turn and glare at him. He wasn't a rag doll, dammit.

"You know the rules," the hunter continued. "If you're wounded, you take care of yourself, or you die."

Evan had been in contact with enough hunters to know that was what they did. They didn't care about each other. There was no sense of found family or camaraderie. Hell, most of the time, it looks like they hated each other. Evan had seen a hunter kill another hunter because of a look. These people were nuts, and he really wished the hunter holding him would let him go.

"Get in the van," the hunter barked.

Orion looked back at the bakery, but it didn't look like anyone would come out, and Orion's father was losing his patience.

"Now!" he yelled, making Evan jump. Did he really have to scream in Evan's ear?

Orion raised his hands in surrender. Evan felt a pang of guilt and sadness. The man had never done anything to him. It looked like he'd cared that Evan was hurt earlier, although that feeling was probably long gone now that he knew that Evan had been baiting him out of the bakery. It would've been nice to have a friend, but Evan had lost his best friend a long time ago.

He wasn't going down that road. He'd tortured himself with thoughts of Davey for years, and he'd promised himself that he would stop. He was sure that Davey had come back for him, and he could only imagine how Davey had felt when he'd found out that Evan was gone. Evan knew his friend, so he was sure that Davey had blamed himself. He hoped he'd stopped, eventually. He hoped that Davey had built a life for himself and that he was happy. Evan couldn't be, and he didn't know anything about Davey's life, but he could allow himself to dream that his best friend had made it even though he hadn't.

Orion finally moved toward the van. Evan's stomach dropped, even though he'd known this was how things would go. Maybe if Orion had been able to run without getting shot, he would have done so, but he couldn't. It was clear that his father would kill him rather than allow him to escape.

The hunter dragged Evan toward the van and pushed him into the back. Evan curled up behind the passenger seat, wondering what Orion would do. He wasn't surprised when Orion climbed into the van, or when the hunter grinned at both of them.

"You two be good in here," he said before slamming the van door shut.

Evan didn't want to be anywhere near him, which meant he had to get away from the passenger seat. He quickly did so, relieved when he managed to do it as the hunter walked around the vehicle. He was wary of Orion, but if he had to choose between him and the hunter, he knew who he'd trust more. Besides, Orion was visibly trying to make himself look smaller, maybe so he wouldn't scare Evan. It was sweet.

"Is he the one who gave you that bruise?" Orion asked softly.

Evan licked his lips and nodded. The hunter wasn't the only one who'd hurt Evan, but Evan didn't think that Orion wanted his life story. Besides, it wasn't a lie. Orion's father *had* hurt him.

"My father's going to hurt me. I don't want you to think it's your fault. It doesn't matter that he used you to get me out of the bakery. You have nothing to do with this, and it's all on his shoulders, all right?"

Evan was stunned by how easily Orion seemed to have forgiven him for baiting him out of the bakery. He wasn't sure how the hunter could be his father because Orion was so different from him. He was sweet and gentle, even though he was big.

Maybe Evan was wrong, but he didn't think so. He didn't think that Orion could hurt a fly. Hell, he was trying to reassure Evan, even though it was kind of Evan's fault that he was here. He wouldn't have left the safety of his bakery if Evan hadn't knocked on his door.

Evan nodded, but before he could say anything, Orion's father climbed into the driver's seat and turned on the engine. Evan pressed his lips together. He still didn't know what the fuck was happening, but whatever it was, he didn't like it.

"We're going to make a few stops," the hunter said. "You two are going to be good and not get anyone's attention because if you do, I'll kill both of you and come back for Perseus. Got it, Orion?"

It was a nice name, and it fit Orion. Evan wondered if the two of them could've been friends if the circumstances had been different. He missed having a friend.

Evan tried finding a more comfortable position, but he didn't think that was possible in the van. His legs hurt from the last beating he'd taken. It would take a while to heal, and in the meantime, he had to deal with the pain.

He caught Orion watching him a few times as they drove, but he didn't say anything. He didn't dare as long as Orion's father was there with them.

Eventually, the hunter parked the van. He didn't say anything as he climbed out and locked the doors, leaving Orion and Evan on their own. The silence between them was heavy, and while Evan wanted to break it, he didn't know how. What was he supposed to do? He could apologize, but Orion had already said that he didn't blame Evan for what happened. He could ask questions, but even though he wanted to know about Orion, none of this would last. Orion would die, Evan would go back to his cage, and after that, to one of the facilities. That was his life.

There was no way out of it, not for him.

"What happened to your leg?" Orion suddenly asked.

Evan blinked. He hadn't realized that Orion had noticed something was wrong with his leg. "I'm fine." There was no reason for Orion to worry about Evan.

"I don't think you are. There's a bruise on your face, and I noticed you were limping."

"I'll *be* fine." Eventually. The doctors tended to allow Evan to heal before they hurt him again. He supposed they didn't want to risk killing him.

Orion didn't look like he believed Evan. Evan thought that was the end of it until Orion opened his mouth again to say the most outlandish thing Evan had ever heard. "I was a hunter once."

Evan's first instinct was to move away, but he had a hard time believing that Orion could hurt him.

"I'm not anymore," Orion quickly added. "I never wanted to be one in the first place, but I was born into it. You know what hunters are, right?"

Evan laughed. He thought it was obvious that he knew what hunters were, considering his situation. "How do you think I got here?"

"I'm really sorry. My father forced me to become a hunter, and I didn't feel I had a way out. For a long time, I didn't. I was a kid, and I would have died out there on my own."

"So you hurt people."

"I did. I also tried to help as many of them as I could. I got hurt in the process, which is how I ended up with the tribe."

Evan had no idea what Orion was talking about. "The tribe?"

"They're a bunch of supernatural people who help guys like you who were captured and hurt. Mostly, they raid the labs and help the survivors."

"I was in a lab once." Evan licked his lips. He wished he had some water, but he doubted that Orion's father would give him anything even if he asked for it. He'd probably hit Evan if he dared try. "I was there for a long time. They moved me around, but the facilities were all the same. They hurt me every time."

"If I'd met you sooner, I would've helped you get away."

"To your tribe?" Evan wasn't sure he believed that. He'd lost hope a long time ago. No one was coming to rescue him. The only person who had was Davey, and he had no way to find Evan. Even Evan didn't know where they were.

"Yeah. I know it sounds weird, but the village became home after they helped me and my brother. My brother found his mate there."

It sounded so easy that Evan *wanted* to believe it. He hoped that Orion wasn't lying to him and that a place like that really existed. "And that was all it took? They didn't care that you were hunters?"

"Oh, it hasn't been easy, and I don't expect it to be in the future. Most tribe members don't trust us, and I don't blame them. Some do, though. Some believed us when we explained that we were forced into it. I know you think it's an excuse, and it probably is a bit, but when you're fourteen and your father tells you that you have to kill someone because it's your duty and that the people we're fighting are monsters, you do what you're told."

"You're not fourteen," Evan pointed out.

"I'm definitely not. I used to do everything my father told me because I was terrified of him and what would happen if I didn't, but as I grew up, I tried to help more people than I hurt. Sometimes, I didn't have a choice, but when I did, I always chose to help people. I still do."

Orion hesitated. Evan wondered why, but he didn't have to wonder for long.

"You wouldn't happen to know someone named Davey, would you?" Orion asked.

Evan stared. There was only one way for Orion to know that name. There was only one way for him to connect Evan to Davey's name. "You know him?"

"Well, I don't know if it's the same guy. He's my mate."

Well, shit. Evan had expected Orion to confirm that he

knew Davey, but that? What the fuck was Evan supposed to do with *that*?

*

Hansen was jolted awake by his phone vibrating on his nightstand. He blindly looked for it, almost knocking it to the floor before wrapping his fingers around it.

"—lo?"

"Something happened. We need everyone at Moore's place," Olga said in an urgent tone, telling Hansen she wasn't kidding.

"I'll be right there."

Hansen hung up and shot out of bed. He wasn't sure how long he'd slept, but the alcohol had left his system, and he felt good enough to fight.

Because that was why Olga had called him. Whatever had happened, she and Moore needed all hands on deck.

Hansen wasn't surprised to find most of the lights in Moore's house were on when he got there and even less surprised to see that almost all of their little group was there. It was a crowd, but they made it work.

Moore glanced around and nodded before turning his

attention to Davey, who stood with Perseus. Hansen didn't see Orion anywhere, which was strange.

"Davey, Perseus, why don't you tell us what happened again?" Moore said.

Hansen sucked in a breath. Why was Davey involved in whatever had happened? It couldn't be good, especially when Orion wasn't around. Hansen's stomach churned with anxiousness.

Davey looked like he was about to puke, but he and Perseus obeyed. They explained that Orion was nowhere to be found and that Davey had smelled someone he thought was Perseus and Orion's father. Everyone in the room knew the man was a hunter, which meant that Orion was in trouble.

"You're sure it was your father?" Olga asked Perseus.

"I'm not sure of anything. I'm not a shifter, so I can't sniff my father. Davey says the scent smells like me and Orion, but different. He explained it's usually a sign of family, and I have to take his word for it."

"I think it's safe to assume that Davey's right," Moore interjected. "If we do, it means that Orion's been with his father for a significant length of time. There's also someone else with them."

"An accomplice?" Rikar asked.

Davey's expression turned shifty. Hansen was going to have to corner him before they left. If there was anything to know about this second person, Hansen wanted to know it before they had to face them.

"Or another victim," Olga offered.

"What do you know?" Moore asked her.

"Not a lot, but I think I can confirm that the person who took Orion is a hunter. I saw a van and Orion with a blond man."

Hansen had always found Olga's gift slightly creepy, even when he was asking her about his mate, but he was glad she could see the future in these situations. She'd saved all of them many times before. It looked like it was Orion's turn now.

"Our main focus will be Orion's father," Moore declared as he took charge of the situation. "We'll have to keep an eye on the man with him, but Davey thought he recognized his best friend's scent, so I think we can assume he's on our side."

Hansen snapped his head toward Davey. Davey's best friend? How was that possible? They'd been talking about Evan just a few hours ago, and he was here? Well, with Orion, and they didn't know where Orion was, but still. Evan was here. It was the closest Davey had been to him since he'd managed to escape. Hansen was ecstatic for his friend but also worried because that meant that they had two people to rescue instead of one, and they still had no idea what they'd be walking into.

"It really depends on what happened to him and how much he suffered," Olga murmured as if she were afraid that Davey would hear her.

Maybe she was. Hansen had only just found out about Evan, but he knew how important the man was to Davey and how messed up Davey probably was right now. They had no idea what state Evan was in, but they all could imagine all too well what he'd gone through.

"Let's assume he's friendly and keep an eye on him in case he attacks," Moore said. "I suppose you're all coming with us?"

Everyone nodded, including Hansen. He wasn't abandoning Davey and Orion.

"Good," Moore continued. "Assuming that Orion's father is taking him back to the hunters, we have to stop them before they get there."

"What are we waiting for, then?" Davey asked.

"We're not waiting. It's time to go and get Orion back."

Everyone moved almost as one, including Hansen. He waited for a few people to pass him by before falling into step with Davey. Davey didn't look at him, but he didn't have to. Davey knew that Hansen would be there for him whatever happened.

They had to walk for a few minutes to reach an area where they could shimmer. Teddy was the first one there, a grim expression on his face as he held out his hands. "Ready?" he asked.

"As ready as we'll ever be," Olga answered.

They reached for Teddy, gripping him where they could. Hansen squeezed his eyes shut because shimmering always made him feel queasy, and he'd need to be ready to act when they landed. Puking in a bush wouldn't help.

It only took a few seconds, and they were wherever Orion was. Hansen blinked his eyes open and tensed, expecting an attack even though he doubted it would come. If Orion and Perseus's father was involved, he was only one man. He was too smart to attack when there were so many of them.

Only two people stood in front of Hansen and the others.

Orion stood in front of an open van. Clearly protecting whoever was inside. His father was in front of him, threatening him. Hansen wasn't sure either of them had noticed they weren't alone anymore.

"Olga, Teddy, take a look around," Moore ordered. "Make sure there are no people hiding in the bushes."

They both nodded and left, but Davey stayed where he was, and so did Hansen. Until Moore gave him orders, he wasn't leaving Davey's side.

Orion was standing up to his father, which was good to see. Hansen didn't know him that well yet, but he knew Orion's history, so he understood how monumental this was for him. Orion and Perseus had always deferred to their father up until they'd left after Orion was wounded. They'd been afraid of him, but Orion could take the asshole. He was taller and broader. He had less experience, but he wasn't alone. He might not know that he was surrounded by allies—which made what he was doing even more impressive—but they were ready for whatever happened.

Perseus stepped forward as if he was about to intervene, but Moore grabbed his shoulder, stopping him. Perseus tried to pull away, but Moore shook his head and kept him where he was. "We're close enough to intervene if we have to, but I think your brother needs to confront your father."

Hansen didn't like standing there and not doing anything any more than Perseus and Davey did, but he understood what Moore was saying. This was probably Orion's only chance to do this.

"Where are your friends?" Orion asked. "How many are supposed to arrive? Will there be enough of them to beat me and my friends?"

Maybe he *had* realized that Hansen and the others were here because it sounded like he was telling them to expect reinforcements. It was smart, and Hansen didn't think that Orion's father realized it.

"We won't allow you to take over the world," the man snarled. "It belongs to humans, not these…these animals."

"Want to know something? Turns out, I'm a wolf shifter's mate."

That had to burn, considering how much Orion's father hated shifters. Both his sons had found their mates and were happy and safe.

Hansen was shocked when the man ran at Orion. He hadn't expected it, but he thought that Orion had because he was ready for his father. He caught the man's fist and swept his legs from under him. As soon as the asshole was on the ground, Orion was on top of him, twisting his arm behind him and pining him to the dirt. Davey sucked in a breath, but he stayed where he was, allowing his mate to finally free himself from his father and the hunters.

Hansen reached for Davey's wrist and gave it a squeeze. "He's fine," he murmured.

"Orion is, but what about Evan?"

CHAPTER TWO

It wasn't that Evan hadn't wanted to help Orion. If there had been anything he could do, he'd have done it. It had been best for him to stay out of Orion's way, though. He wasn't a fighter even when he was in his best shape, and he hadn't been in years. The docs in the labs were careful to keep him alive, but that didn't mean they wanted him to thrive or be strong enough to rebel.

The only thing Evan could do was watch Orion confront his father, and that was what he did. Orion was strong and knocked his father down, and it took everything Evan had not to start cheering. He might be scared, but watching a hunter get his ass handed to him was always a good thing, especially when it was by the good guys.

Orion let go of his father. Evan sucked in a breath because he could see that the asshole was still conscious, but Orion didn't seem to care as he turned toward the van where Evan was huddled and raised his hands, maybe to show Evan he wouldn't hurt him.

"Are you all right?" Orion asked.

Evan nodded. He couldn't look away from Orion's father. Why wasn't he getting up? Had Orion hurt him so badly that he couldn't, or was he biding his time until he could surprise Orion? Evan wouldn't put it past him.

"You think you can come out of the van?" Orion asked, snagging Evan's attention again.

Evan hesitated. "I don't know. I'm scared." He wasn't getting anywhere near Orion's father. That man was vicious.

"It's all right to be scared."

Evan almost snorted. Of course Orion thought it was all right to be scared. "You weren't."

"Oh, I was. I was terrified, Evan."

"You didn't look scared."

"I knew what my father would do. I was prepared, and besides, I had to protect you. No matter how scared I was, I couldn't listen to the fear."

Evan almost moved forward when he noticed someone moving close to the van. It wasn't Orion, and Orion's father was still down. No, this was someone else, someone Evan didn't know and probably couldn't trust. He glanced around, not surprised to see there was more than one someone. Had more hunters arrived? Orion's father had said they would, but Evan had thought he was bluffing. Maybe he hadn't been. Maybe Evan and Orion were about to be carted off to the closest lab. Evan should be resigned because this was what his life had been for who knew how long, but for a moment, he'd thought things would finally change.

"These are my friends, so you don't have to be afraid of them," Orion said gently. "Remember I told you they would come for me? Well, they did, and they'll help you, too."

Not hunters, then. That was a good thing, although Evan still wasn't sure he should trust Orion and his friends. Orion had saved him, but it was a byproduct of Orion kicking his father's ass. It had nothing to do with Evan.

But Orion had been nice to him when he didn't have to. He'd been worried that Evan was hurt, and when his father had tried forcing both of them out of the van, Orion had stood up for Evan and protected him. If there was one person Evan could trust, it had to be him, right? Besides, he was Davey's mate.

Evan still couldn't believe that. What were the odds that he'd be involved in the kidnapping of his long-lost best friend's mate? Fate had to have a sense of humor. The only thing missing was for Evan to find his own mate and for him to be Davey's brother or something. It wasn't possible because Evan already knew that Davey's brother wasn't his mate, so maybe a friend?

Evan had a decision to make. He couldn't stay in the van forever. He had to trust Orion, if anything because Davey's mate wouldn't hurt him.

"Really?" he asked. He still wasn't convinced that these people—whoever they were—would help him, but if Davey was involved, if he was here, then Evan was safe.

He reached out to take Orion's hand when Orion offered it to him. It felt like a monumental step, and it took Evan's breath away, but he did it.

Then Orion's father got up.

Evan scrambled back because there was no way he was getting involved with the asshole. Orion should have killed him when he had the chance, but he hadn't, and now, his father would hurt both of them.

Evan should have known better than to hope. He'd done so for months, but he'd still been trapped and used and hurt. Nothing would ever change. It was too late.

The man had managed to get to his feet, but that was as far as he went before a weird watery substance engulfed him. Evan blinked, wondering what the fuck was happening now and if it was contagious.

That was when his world shook again.

Davey appeared behind Orion's father. Evan hadn't seen him in years, probably — he really ought to find out how long he'd been trapped in various labs — and he looked so good that Evan wanted to cry. They'd been barely more than kids when they'd been forced to separate, and the years showed on Davey's face, but it was him, and that was all that mattered. Evan doubted he looked anything like he had when they were younger, considering everything he'd been through.

"Do you know how much humidity there is in the air right now?" Davey asked as he moved toward Orion's father. "Enough to surround you with water. Enough to drown you."

Evan sucked in a breath behind Orion. What the hell was Davey talking about? Was he the one doing that? How? What was it? What the fuck had happened to Davey?

"Is that what you want me to do?" Davey stopped in front of Orion's father. "I wouldn't regret it. I know what you did to your sons, and one of them is my mate. I'd do anything to have you out of Orion's life, including killing you. You don't deserve to live, anyway."

Evan shivered. His best friend had changed. He never would have spoken that way before, but whatever had happened to him since they'd last seen each other, it had hardened him. Evan supposed that the same could be said about him. He wasn't the same Evan he'd been before, and he never would be again.

"That's not for you to decide," Orion's father said.

He sounded scared, which made Evan feel good. Then he felt guilty for feeling good that someone was scared, but should he? Orion's father was a hunter. He'd probably kidnapped and hurt dozens of people, if not more. He'd hurt Evan, and he would have done much worse if Orion hadn't stood up to him and if Orion's friends and Davey hadn't intervened.

Orion hadn't killed his father. Evan wasn't sure he had it in him. He was a sweet man, no matter who had fathered him.

But Davey wasn't Orion or Perseus. The Davey Evan had known wouldn't have hurt a fly, but Davey wasn't that person anymore. Evan didn't know this Davey. Maybe he'd kill Orion's father.

Evan wanted to see what was happening better, so he moved closer to Orion. He stayed in the van, just in case, but he didn't think anyone would hurt him with Davey there.

"He was going to attack you from behind," Evan told Orion.

"Good thing my mate stepped in, then," Orion murmured back.

Evan had wanted to believe him, but part of him had been hesitant. He wasn't anymore. That really was Davey, and it looked like he was here to save Orion. "You weren't lying. You really are Davey's mate."

"I am, and he'll be over the moon to find you here. He's been looking for you. He never stopped."

Evan smiled. He'd known Davey had never stopped looking for him. He wouldn't have if their roles had been reversed and Davey had been the one left behind. "I never expected him to stop. I'm just not sure what to do. It's been so long, and I feel like my life back then doesn't even belong to me. It's like it was a dream."

Or maybe the past few years or so of his life were the dream—the nightmare. Evan wasn't even sure who he was anymore.

Orion turned to look at him. "Well, if it was a dream, you're still living it. You're free, Evan. You're free, and you have Davey back."

Evan stared at him. He was right. Evan *was* free. He was finally free, and he had no idea what to do with that.

*

Hansen almost felt like he was out of place here. This felt like a family matter that only Orion, Perseus, Davey, and their father should be involved in—and maybe Davey's best friend, who was still in the van and was talking to Orion.

Hansen hadn't seen a lot of Evan yet, but what he had seen worried him. Even though Evan was buried in an oversized hoodie, it was clear that the man needed medical attention and food. When he and Davey had been separated, Evan had been in a lab, and Hansen suspected that was where he'd spent the best part of his time since then. He didn't know why Evan wasn't there right now, but it was a good thing.

Orion and Perseus's father was done for, and Hansen was glad when Teddy grabbed the asshole and shimmered him away. He hoped they would never have to worry about him again.

The reunion between Davey and Evan had almost everyone crying. The danger wasn't over, though. Orion's father had let it slip that more hunters were coming, which meant they needed to be ready for that and that they had to get Evan out of there. Hansen was relieved when Moore ordered Orion and Davey to leave, too. Those two deserved some time to themselves, and Davey needed time with Evan.

When Teddy reappeared, he was ready to take the three of them away. Hansen moved forward to tell Orion that he was glad to have him back, but he froze when he got closer. He looked around frantically, trying to find the person from whom the scent came. There was only one option, but it couldn't be true, could it?

After desperately wanting to find his mate, after wondering when it would happen or if it would happen at all, Hansen had finally met the man of his destiny.

Davey's best friend.

Hansen's mouth went dry as he watched Evan lean against Davey's side. He desperately wanted to go with them, but he couldn't. He'd need to tell Moore why he wanted to, and he wasn't sure it was the best idea.

Evan had already gone through so much. He hadn't only spent years in a cage. He'd also been dragged around by Orion's father, had no doubt been threatened, and he'd been hurt. The bruise on his face made that evident. If Orion's father hadn't been taken care of already, Hansen might have begged Moore for a few minutes with him.

Now wasn't the time for Hansen to tell Evan who he was. He hadn't asked Davey if Evan was a shifter, but just in case, he decided to stay away. Evan didn't need to be shocked. He needed rest, food, a healer, and to spend time with Davey. He needed to reunite with his family and allow himself to live, something he hadn't been able to do since he'd been kidnapped.

Hansen had wanted to meet his mate, and he had. No matter how much he wanted to talk to Evan, he needed to think about what was best for the man, and it wasn't Hansen, not right now anyway.

That was why Hansen forced himself to stay back and watched as Teddy shimmered Evan away. Hansen allowed himself to relax once his mate was gone, but it wasn't easy. His lion was pushing at him to follow. Hansen wanted to, but his priority was to keep Evan safe, which meant getting rid of the incoming hunters.

He turned toward Moore, who was talking to Olga. Their conversation didn't last long. They snapped out their orders, and by the time the hunters arrived, the mutants were ready for them.

They allowed the hunters to move close enough to check the van. From what Hansen could hear, the hunters were wondering what was up with Mitchell. One of them made a joke that Mitchell was probably passed out drunk, and that was why he wasn't answering his phone. All in all, the hunters didn't seem to be taking this seriously, which wasn't surprising.

That was their first mistake. Their second mistake was staying and fighting once Moore stepped forward.

Some hunters were true fighters. They honed their skills, and they were ready for anything, but most hunters were lazy. They thought that capturing a few people and handing them to the labs made them strong, but it just made them monsters. They also didn't usually fight against people who'd spent time in the labs they worked for. They weren't prepared for the abilities the doctors had created.

The mutants knew that, and they took advantage of it. That included Hansen, who grinned fiercely as he used his cloaking ability to hide from their enemies. It meant he could move between them without having to fear they'd attack him and that he could ambush them.

Like always, the first thing he did was get a headcount. Once he had one, he rushed back to Moore, who made the decisions.

Hansen was distracted. Even though he needed to focus, he couldn't stop thinking about Evan. What was he doing right now? Was Davey taking good care of him? The only possible answer to that question was yes, but Hansen still felt the need to check on Evan himself. He didn't think he'd be able to relax until he did.

He sucked in a breath when a fist landed on the side of his jaw. It hurt, but not as much as it would have if he hadn't managed to duck out of the way before it fully reached him. He threw himself at the hunter, slamming the man against the closest tree. When the man continued moving, Hansen kneed him in the guts, then punched him in the face.

"I was starting to think that you'd allow that asshole to get the better of you," Matthew said as he poked at the fallen hunter with his foot. A small crackle of electricity jumped from Matthew's body to the hunter, shocking the man. Hansen felt the hunter was lucky he couldn't feel much right now.

"Stop that," he scolded Matthew. "The guy might be an asshole, but he's unconscious."

Matthew huffed. "What good is my electricity thingy if I can't use it on my enemies?"

"That's something you need to talk to with Moore. I just follow orders."

"You're boring."

Hansen probably was, but he had a secret that was anything but boring. He opened his mouth to tell Matthew that, but he snapped it shut because he didn't know if Evan would want him to tell anyone. Maybe Hansen should keep this to himself until he could talk to Evan.

Of course, Matthew noticed something was up. His eyes sparkled as he gently kicked the hunter again. "What's up with you?" he asked, staring at Hansen.

"None of your business."

"You're my friend. Whatever happens to you is my business. Now spill."

Hansen hesitated, then shook his head. "We'll talk tomorrow. We need to finish this job first."

Matthew pouted. "You're no fun, but fine. Don't think I won't hunt you down if you don't tell me tomorrow, though."

When Matthew wanted answers, he got them by whatever means necessary. Hansen knew better than to try avoiding his friend. It never ended well.

"I know," he told Matthew before pushing him away from the hunter. Matthew was going to give the guy a heart attack if he continued poking at him.

By the time they were done, there were no hunters standing. Some of them were unconscious, but most had been gathered by the van so they could be taken away. The council would take care of them, although Hansen suspected that Orion's father would be a different matter, but the man wasn't his mess to deal with.

He frowned as he pushed one of the hunters toward Elsa, one of the Nix who would transport the hunters to wherever the council would be keeping them. It *was* kind of Hansen's business, though, wasn't it? He was Evan's mate, and Evan was close to Davey, maybe as close as a brother. Orion was Davey's mate, so even though they weren't actually related, they kind of were family. More than that, Orion was Davey's mate, and Davey was Hansen's friend. That was why Hansen worried and why he cared.

He shook his head. He shouldn't have started thinking about family before he talked to Evan. He didn't know what would happen between them. Maybe Evan wouldn't want him. Maybe he'd need time after everything that had happened to him.

Or maybe he'd be happy to meet Hansen, and Hansen would finally get his happy ever after.

*

Saying that Evan was overwhelmed would be an understatement. He'd blown past overwhelmed last night when he'd arrived at the village. He was in freak out, screaming into his pillow territory now, and he had no idea how to deal with it.

He knew he could tell Davey and Orion that he needed

some peace, and they'd do whatever they could to give it to him. He didn't want to bother them, though, and he understood that meeting the leader of the village and the person who was apparently Davey's boss was important. There was a lot that Evan needed to wrap his mind around, though, and he wasn't sure that cramming all of this into his brain the day after he'd been rescued after years of captivity was the best idea.

Rikar was still talking and had a gentle smile on his face. Evan couldn't help but smile back. Orion had promised that the village and the tribe would welcome him, but Evan hadn't been sure he could believe him. Clearly, he should have because Rikar hadn't even hesitated before welcoming Evan into his tribe.

"We can give you your own place," Rikar said.

"That sounds like a bad idea right now."

If Rikar was surprised by Evan's words, he didn't show it. "Whatever you need. We're used to dealing with survivors and helping them get back on their feet. You won't find a better place to do that than here."

"I don't know what I want right now."

"Which is understandable," Moore, Davey's boss, said.

Davey had explained to Evan that by the time he'd managed to escape the lab, it had been too late for him. He'd already been altered in a way that would never change. Evan suspected the same went for him, but he'd decided not to think about it, and that was what he was doing. He'd have plenty of time later. Right now, he wanted to focus on settling down, spending time with Davey, and talking to his family.

Davey had been vague yesterday when Evan had asked about them, so Evan would need answers. He understood that all of this was as much of a shock for Davey as it had been for him. They both needed a little time to wrap their mind around everything.

"What he needs is time," Davey declared. "He can stay with Orion and me for as long as he needs."

"Of course," Rikar said with a nod. "And if any of you need anything, you know where to find me."

Evan did because Rikar was the leader and had made sure to explain which house was his, so Evan would know.

Evan was relieved when the two finally left. Davey and Orion walked them to the front door, but Evan stayed where he was. He closed his eyes and leaned back against the couch, taking a deep breath, then another.

Everything was weird. He kept expecting to wake up and find himself in his cage back in the lab. It wouldn't be the first time he dreamed of being rescued, but it was the only time he'd actually *been* rescued. He wasn't in the lab anymore, and he was never going back.

He'd rather die.

He didn't know how long it would take him to feel better about this entire situation, but he couldn't wait. He wanted to leave the labs behind. He wanted to start living the life he'd been missing out on for so long. Davey hadn't told him how long yet—he was probably scared that Evan would freak out when he found out—but he'd confirmed it had been a long time.

For now, Evan would stay with Davey and Orion in the village. Part of him wondered if he truly belonged here. From what Moore and Rikar had explained, this tribe was full of people who'd been rescued from labs, but even though Evan should feel like he was home, he wasn't sure he was. He didn't want to leave Davey so soon after finally finding him again, though. He just didn't know if this was where he should settle down.

The problem was that the thought of going home terrified

him. That was where he'd been taken, so what was to say that he wouldn't be taken again? The village was a safe place. It was protected, and no hunter would come anywhere near Evan as long as he was here. Maybe he should stay.

And maybe he should stop obsessing over his future and give himself time to breathe.

"How are you doing?" Orion asked.

Evan opened his eyes to find him leaning against the doorframe, his massive arms crossed over his chest. Orion's expression was gentle, as if he were afraid that Evan would break into pieces if he pushed.

Considering how Evan felt, he just might.

"I'm fine," he reassured Orion.

"Physically, sure. What about everything else?"

"I don't know how to answer that."

Orion nodded. "I get it."

"I don't know if anyone can get it."

"Well, Davey spent time in a lab, too. Every mutant who lives in the village has."

It was sad to think that the hunters and the doctors they worked with had hurt enough people to fill a village. "It's not the same."

"I agree. No two experiences are the same, but that doesn't mean you can't find common ground."

"I just need time."

"And you have it. You have as much time as you need and want."

That was the one thing that made Evan feel better. He might not know where he belonged or where to start, but he knew that he'd always have a safe space with Davey. He didn't have to rush into anything because Davey was there for him. Orion, too, and apparently, an entire village full of people.

Someone knocked on the door. Evan groaned, hoping that whoever was there wasn't here for him. He'd already met Rikar and Moore. Who else did he have to meet? The local sheriff? Did the village even have a sheriff or a figure of authority who wasn't one of the two men Evan had already talked to?

"You don't have to talk to anyone if you don't want to," Orion said. "Besides, I don't think that this person is here for you."

"I sure hope not. I don't know anyone in the village."

"No, but people will be curious about you. Word about

what happened yesterday with the hunters has gone out."

"I wasn't there, so I don't know anything."

"You know that's not going to stop them." Orion looked behind himself. "But like I said, Hansen isn't here for you."

Evan tried to place the name, but he couldn't. "I don't know who that is."

"A close friend of Davey. He's a mutant, too."

A shiver slid down Evan's spine. Was *he* a mutant, too? There was a good chance that he was, but that was a problem for the Evan of tomorrow. "I'm glad to know that Davey wasn't alone all this time. He has the tendency of isolating himself when he feels guilty." And there was no way Davey hadn't felt guilty about not being able to help Evan.

"He does. He's in a good place right now, though, especially with you back in his life."

Evan got to his feet and stretched. He was glad that Davey had friends, but right now, Evan's best friend was the pillow he'd used last night. "I'm going to go upstairs."

"Do you want me to call you when dinner is ready?"

"That would be great."

Orion patted Evan's shoulder as Evan walked past him. The casual movement startled Evan. It had been so long since anyone had touched him like that—easily, friendly, with no painful purpose. That was something else he'd need time to get used to again.

He stepped into the entrance and smiled at Davey, who was talking to a man Evan vaguely remembered seeing yesterday. The man's blond hair was cut short, and his brown eyes were warm as they stopped on Evan. The man smiled, and Evan grinned back at the sight of his canines. They were pronounced, almost like a vampire's. It shouldn't be adorable, but it was, and Evan had to resist the urge to poke at one of them.

"I'm going upstairs to take a nap," he told Davey.

"Of course. Let me know if you need anything."

Evan moved to walk past the two, only to freeze when a scent he'd never smelled before reached his nose.

His wolf howled in the back of his head. It was happy because they'd found their mate, but Evan didn't know how to react.

So, of course, he panicked.

*

Hansen could tell the moment everything went wrong. This

53

wasn't what he'd planned, but then, he hadn't really planned anything, had he? He'd been dying to know how Evan was doing, and instead of calling Davey to check in on both of them, he'd decided to show up at Davey's house. He'd hoped to get a glimpse of his mate, and he had.

He hadn't expected his mate to come anywhere near him, though, which was where the problem started.

Evan's eyes widened, and he stumbled back, hitting the railing. He paled so quickly that Hansen expected him to faint, but when Davey reached for Evan, Evan slapped his hand away, shocking all three of them. Evan sucked in a breath, then stopped breathing entirely as he continued staring at Hansen.

"What's going on?" Davey asked, panic coloring his words.

Hansen wasn't sure how to answer that question. Should he tell Davey that he was Evan's mate? It didn't matter that Evan was panicking at the thought of meeting him. Hansen wasn't offended, nor did he believe that it meant that things between them couldn't work. He'd wanted to give Evan time for a reason.

He'd messed up.

He should've stayed away, but it was too late for that. Hansen needed to act, and while he should probably think instead of doing what his instincts were pushing him to do, he didn't resist.

Evan wasn't breathing. Davey was panicking. Hansen had no idea what Orion was doing, but right now, he didn't care.

When he reached for Evan, Evan didn't push him away. He allowed Hansen to pull him into his arms and hold him close. Hansen tucked Evan's face against his own neck, hoping that his scent would calm down his mate enough for him to breathe. It might not be the best idea since Evan had started panicking when he'd realized that Hansen was his mate, but Hansen couldn't think of anything else.

He finally felt Evan suck in a deep breath. He allowed his shoulders to slump and held Evan more tightly against his chest, knowing he couldn't let go of his mate until Evan told him he was ready for it. Thankfully, Davey didn't interrupt. He was watching them with wide eyes. His mouth was slightly open, and his skin was almost as pale as Evan's.

Hansen rubbed his hand up and down Evan's back. It was good to feel his mate breathe. It was good that everyone was relaxing and that Evan wouldn't be running out of here screaming.

"Do I want to know what's going on?" Orion asked.

Hansen blinked at him. Orion was standing next to Davey, but Hansen hadn't noticed him come closer. He was too distracted by Evan.

"I want to know," Davey said. Now that he could see that Evan would be okay, he appeared worried rather than shocked.

"We'll explain," Hansen promised. "Just give him time."

"Time for what? Why did seeing you send my best friend into a panic? What did you do?"

"He didn't do anything," Evan muttered, his face still pressed against Hansen's neck.

"It doesn't look like it to me. What's going on?"

Evan sighed so heavily that Hansen felt his chest move. Evan leaned away, and even though Hansen didn't want to, he had to let him go. Thankfully, Evan didn't go far. He just turned into Hansen's arms so he could look at his best friend. Hansen took the opportunity to wrap his arms around Evan's waist. He didn't miss the way Orion's eyebrows shot up on his forehead or the fact that Davey looked like he wanted to shake him.

"Hansen's my mate," Evan said, going straight to the point.

For a few seconds, nothing happened. Orion and Davey stared while Hansen wondered if Davey would be angry.

Hansen didn't know why Davey should be, but he was protective of Evan. Maybe he didn't think that Hansen was good enough for his best friend. If that was the case, Hansen would show him that he was wrong.

"I don't know what to say," Davey eventually said.

Evan snorted. "How about *congratulations*? How about *I'm happy for you*?"

"Well, of course I'm happy for you. I just didn't expect it."

"You think I did? I spent years in a cage. The last thing I expected was to meet my mate as soon as I stepped out of it." He turned his head to look at Hansen. "It's a lot."

Hansen couldn't help but smile. Even though Evan sounded confused, he wanted Davey to congratulate him. That had to mean that he was happy, right? "I know. I realized yesterday, but I wasn't sure what to do."

"You didn't tell me."

"Considering everything that was happening and the fact that more hunters were coming, I thought it would be better to give you space."

"I want to argue that, but I'm pretty sure that finding my mate would've been the thing that drove me to the edge. You were right not to talk to me right away, but I can still feel disappointed."

"You can feel disappointed by whatever you want. I'm sorry if I overstepped, but I'd do it again if it meant keeping you safe and happy." Hansen wasn't kidding. He wanted Evan to be happy, even if they were never together.

He hoped it wouldn't come to that.

"Well, congratulations," Orion said as he put a hand on Davey's shoulder. "You two have things to talk about, so Davey and I will head to the kitchen to get started on dinner. Yell if you need anything, all right?"

"You can't force me to leave," Davey grumbled, but he allowed Orion to turn him in the direction of the kitchen.

"I'm not forcing you to do anything." Orion grinned at Hansen. "I'm assuming you'll stay for dinner?"

Hansen didn't know. He wanted to stay, and not only because of Evan. He wanted to spend time with Davey. What if Evan didn't want him here, though? He seemed more relaxed now, and he was still in Hansen's arms, but he might change his mind after they talked.

"He'll stay," Evan confirmed.

"Good. We'll see you two later. Evan, you can use the living room if you don't want Hansen in your bedroom."

Evan waited until Orion and Davey were gone—although Hansen could still hear Davey grumbling—to step out of Hansen's arms and turn to face him. Hansen let him go, even though he didn't want to.

"I don't want you to get offended, but I'd like to do this in the living room."

"I'm not offended."

"Good." Evan rubbed his face with a hand. "I'm not gonna lie. This is a lot."

"I know, and we can take this as slowly as you need. My main goal here is to keep you happy and safe."

"Considering what happened to me over the past few years, it's hard to believe I can be either of those things."

Hansen knew how that felt. He followed Evan into the living room and made sure not to sit too close to him. He and Evan might have been through something similar, but Hansen had been out for longer. He remembered how life was right after he'd regained his freedom, and he wanted Evan to feel that he was in control.

59

Evan *was* in control.

"I don't know anything about you," Evan started.

"We'll get to know each other over time."

"But you're like Davey, right?"

Hansen wasn't sure what he meant. "You mean that I'm a mutant?"

Evan grimaced. "I don't know if I like that word."

"It takes a bit to get used to, but it's what we are. We mutated into something different, something that's not quite human and not quite shifter. Yes, I'm like Davey. I have a cloaking ability that means that I can hide in plain sight."

Evan hesitated. Hansen desperately wanted to know what was on his mind, but he wasn't about to push.

"What do you think I would be able to do if I were a mutant?"

Hansen's stomach dropped. "You think you're a mutant?"

Evan's eyes were wide when he looked at Hansen. "I think it's a possibility. I don't know how to feel about it. I barely even remember who I was before the labs. How am I supposed to deal with the knowledge that they changed me so much that I now have abilities no one else has?"

Even though he didn't know how Evan would react,

Hansen reached out to take his hand. He was relieved when Evan didn't push him away. "Whatever you are now, we'll deal with it. You won't find a better group of people to help you through this. We know how it feels. We understand."

"Plus, you're my mate," Evan said with a tearful smile.

"I'd support you through this even if you weren't, but yes. You're my mate, and that matters to me."

"It matters to me, too."

CHAPTER THREE

Evan thought he was putting up a good front. At the
very least, no one had called him out on the fact that
he was freaking out on the inside since he'd arrived at
the village. Not even Davey had noticed, which felt
like a victory.

It shouldn't. Davey would want Evan to talk to him about
how he felt, especially since he was so overwhelmed. Evan
couldn't do that. They'd talked a bit, so Evan knew that his
best friend had blamed himself for not being able to rescue
him. Now that he was free, he wanted Davey to focus on his
own life.

Davey had a home here. He had friends and a mate, and now, he had Evan. He deserved to be happy, and Evan wanted him to be.

What Davey didn't deserve was to shoulder all of Evan's problems. Evan wasn't sure he was up to dealing with them on his own, but he'd been trying.

He looked up and plastered a smile on his face when the bakery door opened. It was a miracle that his smile didn't fall when Davey stepped in.

"Let me guess," Evan said before Davey could ask how he was. "You're here to see Orion?"

Davey's cheeks flushed. It looked good on him, and Evan wanted to keep the smile on his friend's face. "If he's not busy."

Evan gestured toward the back door. "You know where to find him."

Davey rushed toward the door, but he paused before stepping through. "How are you doing?"

Dammit. Evan thought he'd gotten away with it. "What do you think? I couldn't be happier."

Evan was certainly happier than he'd been when he was stuck in a cage. He was still living with Orion and Davey, but he knew that he just had to ask if he wanted his own place. He had Davey back. He even had a job, and he loved helping Orion at the bakery. He'd had dreams before he was kidnapped, but now, the only thing he wanted to focus on was peace. Working at the bakery was peaceful, and he needed more of that in his life.

Davey didn't look convinced, and Evan was already dreading the conversation that was coming. Thankfully for him, Orion had heard his mate, and he was as impatient as Davey.

"Are you coming in or what?" he called out.

Davey looked torn, so Evan strode toward him and pushed him through the door. "Spend time with your mate."

"You were always bossy," Davey grumbled.

"That's because I know what's best for you."

"Do you also know what's best for you?"

That was a heavy question that Evan didn't know how to answer. "I'll figure it out. Go."

Davey obeyed, leaving Evan alone. Evan glanced around the shop, but it was empty of customers for now. The lunch rush hour was long gone, and while some people would come around to grab something for dinner, the busiest part of the day was over.

He grabbed cleaning products and walked around the counter to clean up the small tables. His thoughts were running, though, and he couldn't stop them.

Evan was settling in at the village. He spent most of his time either here at the bakery or in the house that Davey and Orion shared, but he'd met people, and he could see himself having a future here. There was also Hansen to consider. All in all, Evan didn't have much to go back to. His old life was just that—old. It didn't belong to him anymore. He wasn't even sure what was left of it.

That would be easy to find out. He could pick up his phone right now and call his family. He could tell them that he was alive and well, that he was safe, and that he was coming to see them. He could tell them that Davey was okay, too, which, apparently, Davey hadn't done.

Evan still had a hard time wrapping his mind around it. Davey had confessed that after he'd escaped, he'd never gone home. He'd never reached out to their families and had never told them that he was safe. They all probably thought that Davey and Evan were dead, considering how long it had been, and Evan still couldn't quite believe it. He understood why Davey hadn't contacted them. He didn't have to ask because he knew Davey.

Davey felt guilty. He'd been too late to save Evan, and knowing him, he thought that Evan's family would blame him. He was blaming himself, after all.

But Evan was back. His parents didn't have to continue believing that he was dead. He wanted to give them that peace of mind, but part of him was also terrified.

He was scared of what had been done to him in the lab. He still wasn't sure whether or not he was a mutant, but he wasn't the man he'd been when he'd been kidnapped. As far as he knew, he might be dangerous to his family, which was one of the reasons he'd felt it was better to keep his distance for now.

It was hell. He wanted to hug his mother. He wanted to hear his father tease him. He wanted his life to go back to normal, but it never would. He had a new normal now, and he wasn't used to it yet, but he would be eventually. He just didn't think he'd feel complete until he had his family back.

Loud laughter made him jump. He turned toward the back door on instinct, then looked away again instantly when he realized he could see Davey and Orion through the small window in the door. They weren't doing anything they shouldn't be doing at work, but it still felt like Evan was invading their personal space.

From what Evan had seen, Davey had to be sitting on one of the counters. Orion was pressed against him, and Davey's arms were around Orion's neck.

They were happy. They looked like they belonged together, and they did.

Could Evan and Hansen have that? They were mates, too, but Evan felt broken. He wasn't sure he'd ever be able to give Hansen what he deserved. He didn't think that would be enough to send Hansen running, but just because they were mates didn't mean the man had to stay.

Hansen would. He and Evan had been talking on the phone and texting, and Evan felt that he was starting to know his mate. Everything Hansen did and said was centered around Evan. He wanted Evan to be happy and feel safe, so much so that sometimes, it was overwhelming. Hansen didn't hover as badly as Davey, but Evan was sure that the instinct to do it was there. Evan hadn't pulled back because he knew that wasn't what Hansen wanted. He really was the perfect man for Evan, but Evan didn't know what to do with that.

More laughter from the kitchen made him roll his eyes. These two needed to get a room before they started fucking in between the pastries.

He put down his cleaning supplies and went to knock on the door. He didn't wait to push it open, grinning when he caught Davey and Orion still kissing. Davey's eyes widened, and he scrambled off the counter.

Sometimes, Evan wished he could read his best friend's mind because he was ridiculous. "Why don't you two go home early?" he suggested.

Davey frowned. "I don't think Orion wants to close the shop just yet."

"Who said anything about closing the shop? I'll stay until close."

"You don't need to do that," Orion said.

Great, he was frowning, too. This wasn't what Evan had been going for. "I know I don't need to do it. I'm offering. You two haven't had time alone since I arrived in town, so you should take advantage of the empty house."

Orion's cheeks flushed. "There's no need for you to do that."

"Maybe not, but I *want* to do it. Besides, don't you want to give me more responsibilities? I need to show you that hiring me was a good idea."

"I already know it was." Orion glanced at Davey. "But we could go home."

"Please do. No one wants to watch you make out over the croissants."

Davey laughed and moved closer to Evan. Once, he would've pulled him into his arms. Now, he patted Evan's shoulder as if he was afraid Evan would break if he tried anything more intense. "Fine. We'll go home, but you have to promise that you'll call if you need anything."

"Yes, Mom. I promise." Evan hoped he wouldn't need to. He had to start standing on his own two feet and stop letting people protect him. That included Davey, but Evan would have a fight on his hands if he pushed his best friend right now.

"I'll be fine," he promised.

He hoped he wasn't lying.

*

Hansen was happy. It had been a long time since he'd felt like this. Hell, there'd been a time when he hadn't thought he could ever be happy again, right after he'd escaped from the lab he'd been locked in. His entire life had changed. *He* had changed. He'd tried so hard to go back to his old life, but it had been impossible because he wasn't the same person as he'd been when he was taken. When he'd finally realized that, he'd thought that his life was over.

That was when he'd found the other mutants. Working with Moore and the others had given him a new purpose, and, slowly, it had given him his new life. Evan felt like the last piece of the puzzle, and Hansen couldn't wait to see what their life would be like once Evan managed to settle down. He didn't care how long it took. He just cared that he had everything he could want.

He'd finally met his mate. It felt incredible and like it couldn't be true, but it was. He wouldn't have to hound Olga so she could tell him when it would happen because it had.

He reached the bakery and pushed the door open, already smiling because he knew he'd find Evan behind the counter. He hadn't been surprised when Evan had started working with Orion. He was starting to get to know his mate, and he understood that Evan needed to get out of the house. Staying there all day, every day, would drive anyone nuts, but especially someone who was trying to forget bad memories. It was better for Evan to have something to do and people to talk to, and the bakery was perfect for that.

Evan was stacking the boxes he and Orion used to pack pastries, but he stopped when he heard the door. He turned, and when his first reaction was to smile, Hansen felt like his heart might be about to beat out of his chest.

"We didn't make plans, did we?" Evan asked.

"We've never made plans, so no."

"Are you saying that I'm a bad mate because I haven't taken you out yet?"

"I wouldn't say *bad*."

Evan grinned, but there was something lurking in his eyes. Hansen opened his mouth to ask what was going on, even though he suspected that Evan was just overwhelmed and still thinking about everything. He didn't get the opportunity to ask because the door opened behind him, and two women came in with a small army of children.

Evan's eyes widened at the sight, and he looked like he was about to run. Hansen didn't blame him. He wouldn't want to deal with one kid, let alone a dozen.

"Do you still have cupcakes?" one of the women asked.

Her hair was ruffled, and there was a streak of something on her cheek. She looked like he was about to collapse.

"*Please* tell me you still have cupcakes," the other woman said. "Janice insisted that she could bake the birthday cake, but it was a disaster, and we need something to celebrate with."

The first woman—probably Janice, considering the way she glared at the second woman—held out a candle. "There. Even one cupcake would be fine."

"I want a cupcake, too," one of the girls said.

"Me, too!" a boy added.

A third child was poking at a potted plant in the corner, while a boy started crying after the girl next to him pulled his hair.

Evan and Hansen looked at each other. Hansen had no idea what to do, and Evan was clearly lost. "You should ask Orion for help," Hansen suggested.

"He's not here. He went home early with Davey."

The crying was getting louder, and Janice looked like she was about to punch the other mother or run out the door. Something needed to be done.

Hansen sucked in a breath. He had no idea what he was

doing, but he wouldn't let Evan face all of this on his own. It might only be a bunch of children, but as far as Hansen was concerned, they were more terrifying than hunters.

He forced himself to smile and turned toward the two mothers. "I'll go check in the back if we have cupcakes."

Janice dropped the candle into Hansen's hands. Thankfully, now that she knew Hansen and Evan were going to try, she turned her attention to the crying boy.

Hansen rushed into the back room, pausing only long enough to tell the child poking at the plant to be careful. He almost cried in relief when he opened the fridge and found a tray of cupcakes. He didn't know if Orion had gotten them ready for tomorrow, but he didn't think Orion would mind if they used them tonight. Hansen would text him to let him know what had happened, just in case.

He grabbed the tray and rejoined Evan. The potted plant was missing a leaf now, and Janice was scolding the child. The crier had stopped crying and was in the other mother's arms, sniffling, but his smile quickly returned when he saw the cupcakes.

Hansen put the tray down on the counter and stuck the candle into one of them. He turned to Evan because he had no idea how much they were supposed to ask for all these cupcakes. How much would that cost?

"You're not lighting the candle?" Janice asked.

"We can provide the cupcakes, but you'll have to take them home to eat them," Hansen quickly said before Evan could offer to have the party at the bakery.

Janice scowled, and when she opened her mouth, Hansen was pretty sure she was about to demand they be allowed to stay. Evan looked on the edge of tears, and Hansen couldn't allow that to happen. It was his job to protect his mate, even from an angry mother.

"That'll be fifty dollars," he quickly said, ignoring Evan when he made a strangled sound.

Hansen didn't look at his mate. He stared at Janice until she finally took out her phone, but he had no idea how to take the payment. Thankfully, Evan was moving again, and by the time Hansen was done packing the cupcakes into one of the boxes Evan kept behind the counter, Janice was ready to go.

Hansen followed the two mothers and their hordes of children to the door, locking it as soon as the last kid was out. He was pretty sure he saw Janice scowl again, but he didn't care. She and the small demons were out, and they weren't coming back in.

Hansen had been at the bakery for only a handful of minutes, yet it had felt like an eternity. He sighed in relief and turned to Evan, a smile already on his lips. The smile vanished when he realized he couldn't see Evan.

"Evan?" he called out.

A hand appeared over the top of the counter. Evan waved, and Hansen rushed to his side, wondering why his mate had curled up on the floor and was hugging his knees. Had something about the situation reminded him of the labs?

"Hey," Hansen said softly as he crouched next to Evan and put a hand on his knee.

"What would I have done if you hadn't been here?" Evan asked.

"Whatever you could."

"I froze. I didn't know what to say."

"You didn't have to because I was there to help."

"What about the next time someone decides to have a party in the bakery? What am I supposed to do?"

"You can either tell them to leave, or you can tell Orion, and he'll do the same."

Evan's eyes were damp. "I don't want to have to rely on

you or Orion. I want to be able to do these things myself."

"You will, eventually. No one expects you to be fine, Evan. We know what you went through, and we understand."

"When will it stop? It's not fair."

Hansen agreed, but life, in general, wasn't fair. They had to deal with whatever was handed to them, even though, in Evan's case, it was harder than what most people would ever go through.

"I don't think it'll ever stop, but I can promise you that whether or not it does, I'll be with you. I'll do everything I can to help you."

To Hansen's surprise, Evan giggled. "You realize you made her pay way too much, right?"

"I have no idea how much cupcakes cost. Besides, she paid the fifty dollars, didn't she?"

"Because she didn't have a choice with all those kids."

Hansen shrugged. "Next time, they'll plan better."

Hansen was glad to see a smile back on Evan's face, and if he had to ask a rude woman to pay way too much for cupcakes to see him smile again, he'd do it again and again.

He'd do pretty much anything for his mate.

Evan wanted to stand on his own two feet, but at the same time, it felt good to have someone take charge and take care of him. For so long, he'd been alone and had to survive on his own. It wouldn't make him weak to allow Hansen to help him, would it?

Evan wasn't sure he had the strength to rebuild his life on his own. He wasn't even sure he wanted to do it. Hansen was his mate, and that meant something, even though Evan didn't know where things between them would go.

He liked Hansen, and he liked him even more after what had happened tonight. Evan had panicked when the two women and children came in, but Hansen had made everything all right. He'd found a solution while Evan had been freaking out, and even though he'd sold the cupcakes Orion had prepared for tomorrow, a sale was a sale.

"So, what's next?" Hansen asked.

"We don't have any more cupcakes to sell."

Hansen laughed. "I'll apologize to Orion. Do you have to stay open much longer?"

Evan hoped not. He was sitting on the floor behind the counter, for fuck's sake. It wasn't sanitary, and after the day he'd had, he felt the need to take a shower and snuggle in bed.

He took his phone out of his pocket and checked the time. "I can close," he said as he started getting to his feet.

Hansen gently pushed him back down. "Or you could guide me through closing, and I could do it for you."

"It's not your job."

"Good thing I'm not doing it to get paid, then. Let me do this for you, Evan."

Evan almost asked him why, but he knew. Ever since they'd found out they were mates, Hansen had been showing up for Evan, even when Evan didn't feel like seeing anyone. He'd texted and called, had given Evan time and space when he needed it, but had been a steady presence that reminded Evan that he wasn't alone.

Evan knew he wasn't, of course. He'd always have Davey, who'd looked for him for years and hadn't allowed himself to be happy until he'd found him. They were still close, but things were different.

Davey had Orion now, and Evan had Hansen.

Evan wasn't in love with Hansen yet, but it would be so easy to fall for the man. Seeing how much he already cared would be enough. He didn't expect anything from Evan, even though he should. Right now, their relationship was unbalanced, and Evan wasn't sure he could fix it before he fixed himself. He didn't want to push Hansen away, and he didn't want to hurt him by asking him to wait for too long.

Hansen booped Evan's nose with his finger. "What's going on in your head?"

"Things I probably shouldn't be thinking about at this hour of the day while sitting on the floor."

"Then don't think about them. Tell me what to do and rest."

"Fine, but I'm not doing it from the floor."

With a chuckle, Hansen straightened up and offered Evan's hand. Evan took it and allowed his mate to help him to his feet and guide him to one of the small tables by the window. He didn't argue when Hansen pushed him into one of the chairs, and for a moment, they stared at each other.

This man was Evan's mate. If Evan played his cards right, Hansen would be in his life until one of them died. If Evan allowed himself to live, he could be the happiest he'd ever been, even before he'd been taken. He hated that it had taken him being kidnapped and tortured to find his mate, but maybe finding Hansen was a way for fate to ask for his forgiveness — for both their forgiveness. Hansen had been in a lab, too. That was probably why he knew what Evan needed. He'd been through what Evan was going through now. He knew how it felt. He could take care of Evan in a way that no one else could.

Evan cleared his throat and started explaining what to do before he did something stupid like kissing Hansen. He *wanted* to kiss his mate, but was now the best moment to do it? Was there a best moment to do it at all? Evan didn't know, but he still felt slightly panicked, and he knew it would be better to give himself time to relax. He didn't want their first kiss to happen when he was about to cry. He wanted to enjoy it and to know it was the beginning of something.

"There's not a lot to do," he said. "I took care of the cleanup earlier, so we just have to lock up the place."

He gave Hansen instructions, and Hansen followed them as if he *was* paid to do it. It was clear that this was important to him because he put a lot of effort into it, which earned him another point in Evan's heart.

Even though Evan had always known that mates existed, he'd never believed in love at first sight. He supposed he still didn't because he hadn't fallen in love with Hansen the first time he'd seen him, but he was developing feelings much faster than he thought possible. Maybe he should have expected it, considering who Hansen was to him. He wasn't just another guy. He was Evan's mate, and both Evan and his wolf wanted more.

Would it be right to start something with Hansen when Evan's life was still a mess? Evan wanted to think it would be, but there was something weighing on him that he felt he should take care of before things got messier with his mate.

"You should probably let Davey know that you're okay," Hansen said as he cleaned the table.

Evan blanked. "Why?"

"I'm sure you remember how much he frets. Orion might have managed to distract him for a bit, but with the bakery closing, he'll start wondering if everything's fine."

Hansen was right, and realizing that was startling. Once, Evan had been the one person who knew Davey best. They'd been inseparable. They'd been childhood friends, attached at the hip since they were six and had met in first grade.

But they hadn't spent time with each other in years. Evan had been utterly alone, but he was glad that Davey hadn't been there. He needed people. Everyone did. It was bad enough that Davey had felt guilty for something he couldn't help. At least he'd had people who loved him.

Evan texted Davey to reassure him that he was okay before Davey could start freaking out. He also teased him a bit about what he'd been up to with Orion, and while he was happy for Davey, he was also slightly uncomfortable at the thought of going home tonight. Surely they'd had their fill of each other by now?

It wasn't like they'd fuck on the coffee table if they hadn't, and it wasn't the first time that Davey had a boyfriend, but Evan felt like the third wheel when he spent too much time with Davey and Orion, especially in the privacy of their home, where they were more relaxed and the PDA was off the charts.

"How's Davey?" Hansen asked.

"Probably blissed out, although he did manage to send me a text. You were right. He was getting worried."

"Would he worry even more if you didn't go home tonight?"

Evan put his phone down and looked up at Hansen. "What are you suggesting?" He wanted to say yes without even thinking about it, but could he?

He wanted everything with Hansen. He wanted what Davey and Orion had, including sex and not being able to stay away from each other for long. It would take time to build up to that, but Evan felt like he and Hansen were ready for something, even though he didn't know what that something was. Spending the night might be a little too fast, though.

"You could give Davey and Orion an evening to themselves, and I could continue taking care of you. If you're okay with it, I'd like to cook you dinner," Hansen offered.

"What about after dinner?"

"Like I said, I want to take care of you, whatever that entails."

Evan bit his lower lip. "That's probably not going to entail sex."

"That's perfectly fine with me. It's not why I asked you to spend the night."

"It's what people will assume we did."

"Do we care about what people will assume? We're mates. People will think that we'll be bonded in a week, anyway. What happens between us when we're in private is no one's business but ours. We can go at whatever pace you feel comfortable with, and I don't care what people think of that."

Evan was rethinking love at first sight because he was already a little in love with this man. "As long as you don't expect anything, I'd be happy to spend the night at your house," Evan said, hoping — knowing — he wasn't making a mistake.

Hansen was the rest of his life, and it looked like the rest of his life was about to start.

*

Hansen wasn't surprised that Evan wasn't ready for the next step. He hadn't expected him to be. He'd been in Evan's place, and he remembered how overwhelming everything was. Evan needed to find his footing and his place in a life he'd missed out on for years. Of course he wasn't ready for anything more with Hansen.

And that was okay. Hansen hadn't been lying when he said that he would give Evan whatever he needed. His instinct was to take care of his mate, of course, but it was more than that. He wanted to take care of Evan because he deserved it after everything, just like all the other survivors had deserved it.

Hansen's job was more on the fighting side of the mission he and the mutants had given themselves, but he'd lived with the tribe long enough to have helped survivors, too. He liked watching them come back to life. He liked seeing them realize that their nightmare was finally over and that the rest of their life was in their hands. It could be terrifying, but also exhilarating.

Evan was free, and with all the support he had, he could do anything he wanted.

"The only thing I expect is that you allow me to take care of you," he promised.

Evan was still fiddling with his phone. He'd checked in with Davey, and since Hansen had no doubt that Davey would freak out if Evan didn't come home tonight, he tilted his chin toward the phone. "You should tell Davey."

Evan groaned. "He's going to freak out."

"Yes, well. He's been overprotective since you arrived."

"I don't blame him. I know he feels guilty, and I'd probably do the same if our roles were reversed. I want to take care of him, too, after the years we spent apart, but he has Orion."

"And you have me."

Evan blinked as if he hadn't remembered that. Hansen didn't think that was the case. It was more that Evan wasn't used to people taking care of him anymore.

"I'll text him."

"He's going to call you right away."

The corners of Evan's lips curled into a smile. "Probably, but that's fine."

Sure enough, Evan's phone started vibrating as soon as he put it down on the table. Evan's smile was more pronounced as he picked it up, answering right away.

"You do know you're not my mother, right?" he asked.

Hansen went back to work with a smile on his face. He loved that Davey was so worried about Evan. He wished it wasn't out of guilt, although he understood that was only part of it. Evan deserved people who cared about him and who could show him that they did.

As Evan had said, there wasn't much left to do. Hansen cleaned the tables and counter again, then checked that everything in the kitchen was turned off. Orion would be at work in a few hours—Hansen wasn't sure how he managed to wake up at three in the morning every day to do this—and when he arrived, he'd find everything clean and neat.

Hansen turned off all the lights, checked that the front door was locked, and turned to Evan. He was still on the phone, softly talking with Davey, but he quickly said goodbye when he realized that Hansen was done.

That was when things turned a little awkward.

Hansen had expected it. He and Evan had never spent the night in the same place, and their relationship was new. Hell, Hansen wasn't even sure he'd call it a relationship. Maybe friendship? He wanted it to be more, but he wasn't about to rush Evan. Maybe they could talk about it over dinner.

"Ready?" he asked.

Evan got to his feet. Hansen gave him space as he finished checking the bakery, keeping an eye open when they stepped into the back alley. Orion and Evan had been here with Orion's father just a few days ago. There weren't good memories here, but Evan didn't seem to be thinking about them. He turned the last light off, closed and locked the door, then checked it again to be sure it was locked.

Hansen wanted his mate to be out of there as soon as possible. He realized that he couldn't protect Evan from memories, and considering that Evan worked here, he probably saw the back alley several times a day, but his lion wanted Evan out of there, and Hansen agreed.

Like everything in the village, Hansen's house wasn't far. It was small, more like a cottage, but he liked it. He was fine with something small since he wasn't planning on having a family. He didn't have experience with kids, and what had happened today had cemented that conviction. He wanted to focus on Evan and their relationship, and he suspected that Evan felt the same way. It was something they needed to talk about, though. If Evan did want kids, they'd have to move.

Evan seemed fascinated by every trinket in the kitchen. As Hansen got things out to make pasta, Evan picked up pictures, poked at objects, and looked out the window.

That was why Hansen didn't expect it when Evan suddenly asked, "Do you think I'm a mutant?"

Hansen put down his wooden spoon and turned to face his mate. He leaned against the counter, trying to find the right words even though he knew they didn't exist.

"You were in the same lab as Davey was until he managed to escape," he said.

Evan nodded. He picked up a picture frame that held a photo of Hansen and the other mutants. It had been taken right after they'd moved to the village, and they all looked happy.

"Davey was already a mutant by the time he escaped," Hansen continued. "We don't know if they did whatever they did to Davey to you, too, but there's a good chance they did." Hansen swallowed. He seldom talked about these things, and he wished he didn't have to, but this was Evan. "From what we were able to understand by putting our stories together, most of the mutants have passed through one specific lab."

"The one where Davey and I were," Evan offered.

"Yeah. We don't know if it was the only lab that did those kinds of experiments, but there's a chance it was."

"Which means that I'm probably a mutant." Evan put down the picture frame. "Why don't I know for sure? Davey does. Shouldn't I know?"

"It really depends on what your ability is. Some are more obvious, like Matthew's, who controls electricity. I knew something was different with me after I escaped from the lab, but I didn't know what that something was until I thought someone was following me and freaked out. They were alarmed when I suddenly disappeared from in front of them."

"You mentioned a cloaking ability."

"I don't turn invisible. If someone really tries looking for me, they can find me, but when we're fighting hunters, they don't have the time to focus on me that way. They also don't expect me to be there, which makes things easier."

"So you think I probably have some kind of ability but don't know about yet."

"I think it's a strong possibility, yes. You don't have to know what you can do, though. You can just ignore all of it until it presents itself."

Evan looked as though he wasn't impressed with that suggestion. "I need to know if I'm dangerous." He hesitated and licked his lips. "I think I'm ready to reach out to my family."

Hansen knew a bit about that situation. Davey had confessed that he'd never contacted his family or Evan's after he escaped from the lab. He'd been focused on finding Evan and feeling guilty about leaving him behind, and he hadn't wanted Evan's family to feel like he was responsible for what had happened.

Maybe now that Evan was back, both Evan and Davey could get their families back. Hansen hoped so. Family was what made life worth living.

"Whatever you need from me, I'll give it to you," Hansen promised.

To his surprise, Evan huffed and moved toward him. Hansen didn't know what to expect, but it wasn't Evan hooking an arm around his neck and pulling him closer so he could press their lips together.

"You shouldn't be this perfect," Evan grumbled.

He didn't move away, and Hansen didn't want him to. "I'm really not."

"I don't know. You look pretty perfect to me."

Since Evan had taken the first step, Hansen decided to take the next. He pulled Evan closer, making sure he could move away if he didn't want this. Evan stayed where he was. He tilted his face and smiled at Hansen, and it was the most natural thing in the world to lean down and kiss him again.

It was soft and gentle, and it was everything Hansen wanted Evan to have. It was the first chapter in what he hoped would be a long love story between them.

It was perfection. It was *them*.

CHAPTER FOUR

Evan had almost changed his mind a dozen times. Was he really doing this? Was he really about to knock on his parents' door?

He stared at the house where he'd grown up. They still lived here. The house looked the same, even though some things were different. There were more flowers in the front yard now. Someone had put a bench there, and Evan could tell his mother spent a lot of time outside. He wondered if she'd started gardening after he vanished. Maybe she needed something to distract herself.

"We can still go back," Davey said as he leaned closer.

They'd asked Teddy, one of the mutants, to shimmer them here. He'd agreed without hesitation. Evan hadn't been surprised. All the mutants were incredibly supportive of him. They understood what he'd gone through.

No one had been more supportive than Hansen, not even Davey, and that was okay. It was how it should be. Davey's life was with Orion, and he shouldn't focus on Evan. Evan had his own mate who did that.

"Or you could take some time to think," Orion said. "Both of you. This impacts you as much as it impacts Evan, Davey."

"I'm here to support Evan," Davey said.

Evan turned to look at him. "You're here to see your family."

"We're standing in front of *your* house."

"As if my mom isn't going to call yours the second she sees us."

Davey looked away. "They may not be friends anymore."

Evan glared at his best friend. "Stop that. They don't know what happened to either of us. Even if they did, they wouldn't blame you for me being taken or for you not being able to rescue me after you escaped. None of this was your fault. You didn't kidnap me, you didn't stick me in a cage, and you didn't torture me. You came back for me. You looked for me for years. You did everything right, and if you don't stop feeling guilty, I'm going to smack you."

Evan half-expected Davey to continue pouting, but instead, he grinned and gently pushed him. "There you are. It's been a while since I saw the real Evan."

Evan had no idea who the real Evan was anymore, but he was starting to find out. He was different from the Evan he'd been before, but it wasn't a bad thing. Now, he was Evan with a mate. He was Evan with a job, where he worked with his best friend's mate. He was Evan, who lived in a tiny village and was building a life there. He was Evan in therapy, which regularly kicked his ass, but he couldn't do without.

His therapist had agreed that if he felt it was time for him to see his parents, he should see them. He didn't know what he was about to walk in on, and he prayed it wouldn't be bad, but he couldn't continue avoiding them. He especially couldn't continue using himself as an excuse.

He might or might not be a mutant. The probability that he was one was high, but so far, he hadn't made anyone explode or anything like that, so he was pretty sure he wouldn't hurt his family. He'd never forgive himself if he did.

He trusted Hansen, Davey, and Orion. If anything weird happened, they'd intervene. That was the only reason Evan was here. The three men with him would be his family, and that made him feel safe.

"I'm scared," he whispered.

Davey took his hand and squeezed. "Me, too, but it's time."

Evan had a choice. He could stay on the sidewalk hiding behind a tree, call Teddy and ask him to pick them back up, or walk away from his hiding place and take the next step in his new life.

He sucked in a breath and rushed forward, not giving himself time to change his mind. He dragged Davey with him, and he was sure that Orion and Hansen weren't far behind.

He didn't hesitate when he reached the front door. He knocked, then squeezed Davey's hand harder. He was glad that Davey was with him, not only because Davey deserved to have his family back, too. Evan wouldn't have wanted anyone else to stand on his parents' porch with him today, not even Hansen. Davey understood. He'd lost as much as Evan had.

Evan started crying as soon as he recognized his mother's footsteps. By the time she opened the door, tears were streaming down his cheeks. For a moment, they stared at each other.

Evan had changed physically as well as mentally. He was older, and he'd been through hell. That showed on his skin. For a second, he was afraid that his mother wouldn't recognize him, but she screamed and threw herself forward, and Evan had to brace himself.

"Evan? Evan!"

Evan's mother clung to him as if she was afraid he'd disappear. Maybe she was. She hadn't seen him in years and probably thought he'd been dead. Instead, he was standing on her porch, very much alive and losing the ability to breathe because she was squeezing him so hard.

He let go of Davey's hand and hugged her back. "I didn't survive for so many years only for you to smother me to death," he teased through his tears.

She let go instantly. "Robert? Robert, you need to come *now*."

Evan's chest squeezed. He missed his father as much as he'd missed his mother.

His mom didn't seem to be able to let him move away because even though she wasn't hugging him anymore, she'd taken his hand and was squeezing it to the point of pain. Evan couldn't find it in himself to complain. He was squeezing back just as hard.

His father appeared from the kitchen. He was frowning, but when he saw Evan, he froze. He wavered and had to lean against the stairs, and Evan was moving forward, letting go of his mother so he could hug his father as fiercely as his mom had hugged him.

"Evan?"

Evan's father wasn't screaming. He sounded like he couldn't believe that Evan was there. To be fair, Evan almost couldn't believe it, either.

"It's me," he confirmed. "I'm home. I'm home."

"What happened to you? Where were you? Are you okay?"

Someone cleared their throat. Evan didn't have to look to know it was Hansen. Even here, he was taking care of Evan.

"Why don't we all sit down?" Hasen suggested.

It was a sign of how overwhelmed Evan's parents were that they didn't question who Hansen was. Hell, Evan's mother barely even looked at him. She'd seen Davey, and she was hugging him to death now.

"My boys are home," she said with a sob.

97

Evan's eyes burned, but he didn't care how much he was crying. He figured he was allowed to today of all days.

Evan was thankful for Hansen and Orion because if it wasn't for them, he, his parents, and Davey would still be crying on the porch. Instead, Orion and Hansen guided them inside the house, found the living room, and helped them sit on the couch. All four of them squeezed on the same one. Evan didn't want to be far from his parents right now.

"I need to call Cynthia," Evan's mother said. "Your mother should be here," she told Davey. "Your father. They all should be here."

Evan had known that would happen. He'd hoped that his and Davey's mother were still close, and he was glad they'd had each other. They'd both lost a son when Evan and Davey had vanished.

"What happened to you?" Evan's father asked.

"Maybe we should wait until Davey's family is here, too," Evan suggested. "I want to tell you everything, but I don't want to have to go through it twice."

His father's expression turned serious. "We're not going to like this, are we?"

"I wouldn't have stayed away for so long if I hadn't been

forced to."

"My poor boy."

Evan started crying again. He'd imagined this day so many times over the years. He hadn't thought he would ever have it, but here he was.

Home.

*

Things stayed pretty normal until more people arrived. Hansen had heard Evan's mother calling Davey's mom, but he hadn't realized that she would bring more people than Davey's father with her.

Everyone was eager to see Evan and Davey. They hadn't seen them in years and hadn't even known that they were alive. It wasn't a surprise to see that everyone wanted to hug and cry on their shoulders.

Hansen and Orion exchanged a glance. They'd been pushed to the side when Davey's mother had barged into the house and thrown herself into her son's arms. Hansen and Orion had stayed there, watching their mates.

"How are you feeling?" Hansen asked Orion. Orion didn't have a family who would be happy to see him. He had his brother, but beyond that, his family was better lost than found. It couldn't be easy for him to watch as Davey and Evan were surrounded by love.

But when Orion smiled, he looked sincere. "I'm happy for him," he said, tilting his chin toward his mate, who had a baby in his arms and was crying.

From what Hansen had gathered, the baby was the son of Davey's younger sister. Davey was an uncle, and he hadn't even known.

Evan was talking with his mother, while Evan's father watched them both. The man was frowning, which was an out-of-place expression. Evan had promised to explain what had happened to him and Davey, and if Hansen had to bet, that was what his father was thinking about.

It wouldn't be easy. Hansen wished Evan didn't have to do it because it would hurt him, but he wouldn't let it stop him. Evan wanted his family to know what had happened to him. It would probably be the last time he talked about it beyond therapy, and that would be perfectly fine.

"Why do you have bodyguards?" Davey's mother suddenly asked.

Davey blinked up at Hansen and Orion. Their hovering

was kind of awkward, but neither of them was willing to get far from their mate.

"They're not bodyguards," Davey said with a smile. He held out his free hand, and Orion moved forward, taking it and linking their fingers together. "This is my mate, Orion."

The level of noise rocketed. Hansen grinned when Orion gave him a slightly panicked look as he was enfolded into Davey's family, but he didn't smile for long because Evan's mother had heard the conversation and was turning her attention to him.

"If Orion is Davey's mate, does that mean this man is yours, Evan?"

"It does," Evan confirmed with a smile that Hansen was pretty sure he'd never seen before. It was bright and wide and went straight to Hansen's heart.

Evan's father cleared his throat. "Why don't we introduce everyone? My name is Roger, and I'm Evan's father. This is my mate, Isabel." He wrapped an arm around his mate's shoulders.

"I'm Hansen," Hansen introduced himself. "Evan's mate."

That still felt weird to say. Hansen had wanted to meet his mate for so long, and now, he had. He was happy, even though he wished things had happened in different circumstances.

Isabel jumped to her feet, and the next thing Hansen knew, she was in his arms.

He exchanged a glance with Evan, who looked amused. Hansen didn't have a problem with hugs, but it was startling because he'd never met Evan's mother before.

"You are *so* welcome into our home," Isabel said, leaning back and looking at Orion. "Both of you. The boys are like brothers. We're all family, and you being Evan's mate means that you are, too."

"They both are," Davey's father declared. He offered Hansen his hand, and Hansen shook it. "I'm Arnold."

"Hansen. It's a pleasure to meet you."

"And this is my wife, Cynthia," Arnold continued. "And our youngest daughter, Ellie. That's her husband, Jack, and their son, David." He pointed at Davey's other sister. "That's Sarah and her mate, Brad."

Hansen could only nod. He was sure Evan and Davey had more family that they'd eventually meet, but for now, even this felt overwhelming.

"So what happened to you two?" Ellie asked after taking

her son back.

Everyone fell silent. Evan looked nervous again, so Hansen sat on the edge of the coffee table. He didn't want to be rude, but his mate mattered more than manners. He'd apologize to Isabel if she wanted him to, but only after Evan was done with this.

"I did say I would explain, didn't I?" Evan said with a small chuckle that held no amusement. "All right. Well, to make a long story short, Davey and I were kidnapped."

Isabel sucked in a breath while Evan's father pressed his lips together. Cynthia was already crying again and clinging to Davey's arm.

"You know about the labs and what happens in them, so I don't have to go into details," Evan continued. "But we both ended up in one of them. The past few years have been hard."

"But you're home. How did you escape?" Roger asked.

"That would be the mutants," Davey said as he smiled at Hansen. "They're a group of people who were once prisoners of the labs, too. They've banded together and have been rescuing people."

That wasn't exactly what had happened to either of them. Hansen wasn't surprised that Evan hadn't yet mentioned that

Davey had managed to escape much sooner than he had. He knew how Davey still felt about that.

"So they saved you?" Cynthia asked.

Davey's smile fell. "Not exactly." He didn't explain, leaving everyone visibly frustrated.

Evan huffed. "Davey doesn't want to tell you what happened because he feels guilty, no matter how many times I tell him that none of this was his fault. He managed to escape a few years ago, but he had to leave me behind. He returned as soon as he could, but I'd already been transferred to another lab by then. He's been looking for me since then and feeling guilty about abandoning me or something like that."

Isabel pressed a hand against her mouth and turned to look at Davey. He was staring at the floor, and his back had gone ramrod straight. It was clear that he expected Evan's parents to blame him for what happened.

"Oh, baby," Isabel said as she got up from the couch and went to hug Davey. "We know you never would've abandoned him. Is that why you didn't come home? Because you thought we would blame you?"

A sob escaped Davey's throat. Hansen felt out of place, even though he was Evan's mate. Maybe only family should be present during this conversation. He supposed that he and Orion were family now anyway, but Davey was vulnerable, and Hansen didn't know if he was comfortable with him being here.

All four parents rushed to Davey's side. He might've been worried about Evan's family blaming him, but it was clear he shouldn't have. Roger and Isabel folded him into their arms as if he were their son.

Hansen took the opportunity to lean closer to Evan, taking his hand and waiting until Evan turned to look at him. "Everything okay?"

Evan's eyes were red but bright. His cheeks were flushed, and he looked more alive than he had since he'd been rescued.

"I'll be fine," Evan promised. "Once this is over, I never want to talk about the labs again, but they need answers."

Hansen raised Evan's hand and kissed his knuckles. "Never talking about the labs might be hard, considering you live in a village full of mutants who rescue survivors from them, but I'll do what I can."

"You know what I mean," Evan said with a glare that was, frankly, adorable.

"You two are wonderful together," Isabel said as she

retook her place next to Evan. "I can't believe my baby is mated."

"Not yet," Evan told her. "Davey was able to escape years ago, but I was stuck in the lab. I was moved several times. When a hunter took me out of my cage, I thought that was what was happening again. I expected to end up in another lab, but instead, the hunter dragged me to this small town, this *village*, really, and forced me to bait his son out of his bakery."

"That baker would be me," Orion said, raising his hand. "My father wasn't happy that me and my brother left him and moved into the village. He tried to use Evan to get to me, and he succeeded, but not for long."

"Orion kicked his ass. That's how I ended up in the village. They took me in, and I've been staying with Davey and Orion since then."

"How did you meet your mate?" Evan's mother asked.

"I'm one of the mutants Davey mentioned earlier," Hansen explained. "I live in the village, too, and work with the others to rescue survivors and close the labs."

Isabel's expression was serious. "You were a prisoner, too?"

"I was, a while ago. I never want anyone to have to go through what I went through, which is why this is important to me."

"You poor boys have been through hell, haven't you?"

Hansen wasn't sure that was what he'd call it, but it wasn't far off.

*

No matter the horrors of the past few years, Evan thought he could forget them if he had all of this.

His mate. His family. Davey.

He'd thought he'd lost all the people he cared about. He'd thought he would die in a lab, sad and alone, without ever seeing any of the people he loved again. He hated Orion's father, but he would always be grateful to the man for taking him out of his cage and giving him all of them back. If it wasn't for him, Evan wouldn't be here. Without knowing it, Orion's father had saved his life, and while Evan hated owing him anything, he was also happy because he knew that Orion's father would hate knowing he was the reason Evan was so happy now.

Evan's mother couldn't seem to stop touching him. She

was holding his hand as she talked to Hansen, and Evan allowed himself to take everything in.

It seemed like Orion and Hansen fit well enough in this family. That was good because Evan wasn't about to let go of either. He wanted Hansen and his family. He wanted to be able to forget all about the labs and focus on his future.

"I hate that you boys had to go through all of that," Cynthia said. "But you're home now."

Evan wiggled on the couch. "Well, we have a new home."

Everyone fell silent. Evan hoped his parents would be happy for him, even though it meant that he wouldn't come back. He was willing to visit and even spend a week or two here, but he was building a life in the village, and he didn't want to stop. Besides, Hansen's home was there. He couldn't just up and leave. He was a part of the team that rescued people from the labs, and Evan didn't want him to stop if he didn't want to. It was important to Hansen, and Hansen was important to Evan.

"Of course you do," his mother said as she gave him a watery smile. "And what your mate is doing is important. We wouldn't want to take either of you away from that."

"And it's not like you can't visit," Cynthia added. "And

maybe we can visit you."

Evan didn't know if that would be possible. They'd have to ask Rikar since he was the leader of the tribe and the kind of mayor of the village.

"Of course," Davey reassured their mothers. "You can visit anytime you want, and we'll give you our phone numbers and everything you need to contact us. We'll visit as often as we can." He hesitated. "I'm on the team, too."

"Does that mean you're a mutant?" his father asked.

Evan hadn't yet mentioned that he probably was one, too. His heart ached at the thought of his parents looking at him differently. He didn't know if he was one for sure, anyway.

That was what he was trying to convince himself of. He knew he *was* a mutant, though. There was no way he wasn't. Even though he was happy, his future would be an uphill battle. He was working with a therapist, but no one went through what he'd gone through and came out on the other side without scars, both physical and mental.

But Evan wouldn't have to do any of this alone. He had his family back, and Hansen wasn't going anywhere.

Davey sucked in a breath. "I am." He raised his hand palm up, and drops of water gathered there, seemingly appearing out of nowhere, causing gasps and little screams of surprise.

Evan had seen his best friend do that before, but he was still impressed.

Davey nodded. "This is what I do. Don't ask me how it works because I don't think anyone knows, but I can manipulate water. It helps when we fight hunters because it includes the water in a human body."

Cynthia pressed a hand over her mouth. "What did they do to you?"

"I never found out," Davey said, still not looking at her. "But whatever it was, it changed me. I decided I might as well use it against them." He closed his hand, and the water vanished into his skin.

"I don't know if I'm a mutant," Evan interjected before he lost his courage. "But there's a good chance that I am. I don't know what I can do, but I'm sure that eventually, I'll find out."

"Will you join the team when you do?" Evan's father asked.

Evan hugged him just because he could. "I don't think so. What they're doing is great and needs to be done, but I don't think I have it in me to go into more labs and face the people who hurt me so badly. Maybe in a few years, I'll change my mind, but for now, I'm happy working at Orion's bakery."

"You have a bakery?" Davey's mother asked Orion.

Evan was glad for the distraction. Orion answered her questions with a smile, and Evan could allow himself to relax and squeeze Hansen's hand.

Hansen was still on the coffee table, ready to intervene if anything happened. He'd been Evan's rock through all of this, something Evan hadn't expected to have.

To be fair, he hadn't ever expected to be free of the labs, either.

"You're happy?" Evan's mother asked him while everyone else listened to Orion.

That was a tricky question to answer. Was he? "I think I'm getting there. I have a lot to deal with, and most days, it's so hard, and I'm not sure why I'm doing it, but then I talk to Orion, or Davey hugs me, and Hansen texts me, and I remember. I'm doing all of this because I deserve it. I can finally live my life. I don't want to miss out on anything."

Evan had already missed out on so much. Ellie was younger than him and Davey, but she had a son. Evan had always loved her like a sister, and he felt like an uncle to her son, and he hated knowing that he and Davey hadn't been there for her. They hadn't been there when she'd met her mate, when they'd gotten married, or during her pregnancy. All of that had been taken from them by the hunters and scientists, and Evan would always hate them for that.

But they couldn't change the past. The only thing he and Davey could do was look to the future and deal with what happened to them. Their past might be messy and awful, but their future wouldn't be. *That* was what they should focus on.

Evan was a different person than he'd been the last time he'd sat on this couch with his parents, but it still felt like coming home. Eventually, his mother got up to get drinks, and when Evan tried to follow her, she pushed him back down and forced Hansen to sit next to him so he could keep an eye on him. Evan could already tell that these two would gang up on him, but that was fine. He'd been without anyone worrying about him for too long.

Hansen wrapped an arm around Evan's shoulders and held him close as Evan glanced around the room. Davey's father had gone to the kitchen, too, and Davey was squeezed between his mother and Ellie. He was holding his baby nephew again, and every so often, he looked down at him with stars in his eyes.

If Davey and Orion didn't have a kid in the next year, Evan would eat his underwear. He was happy for his best friend. Evan couldn't even imagine having kids, but it was obvious that Davey had. He'd pressed pause on his life for years. He'd been focused on finding Evan and feeling guilty, and that was where all his attention had gone. Even after meeting Orion, Evan had never been far from Davey's mind.

Evan was back. Davey didn't have to worry about him anymore, and if Hansen had anything to say about it, he never would. Worrying about Evan was Hansen's job now, which meant that Davey could focus on what came next for him and Orion.

Evan believed that was kids, and he'd happily be Uncle Evan whenever it happened.

*

The evening sun cast a golden hue over Hansen's home, illuminating the living room in a soft, inviting glow that he hoped would help Evan relax. Evan stood at the living room door, looking hesitant.

"Are you sure you're fine with me spending the night

again?" he asked.

The last few weeks had been a whirlwind for him, and Hansen wasn't surprised that he needed reassurance, especially after the day he'd had. "You're always welcome in my home, Evan."

"Because I'm your mate."

"And because I like you."

Evan's lips curled. "You like me because I'm your mate."

"And because you're brave, caring, strong, and resilient. Come in, Evan," Hansen tried to keep his voice soft and soothing. He wanted Evan to feel at home here. He hoped that, eventually, it *would* become his home.

Evan nodded, but he was still fiddling with the hem of his shirt. Hansen didn't expect him to feel fully comfortable here yet, and staring at him wouldn't help, so he smiled at his mate. "I'll get started on dinner." After the emotions of the day, Evan had to be hungry.

Evan and Davey's families had tried convincing all four of them to stick around for dinner, but Evan had insisted he wanted to come back to the village. No one had pushed, which told Hansen that they knew Evan's limits, even though they hadn't seen him in years. Davey and Orion had returned with them, but they'd gone home. Evan had wanted to give them space, and Hansen had been delighted when he'd asked if he could spend the night at his house again. He hadn't hesitated to say yes. He was glad that Evan considered his home a safe place.

Evan followed Hansen into the kitchen. Hansen had planned ahead, even though he hadn't known how the day would go. He'd suspected Evan would need comfort food, so he'd prepped everything he could and had left it in the fridge.

"I'm making your favorite," he said. "Chicken Alfredo." Evan had mentioned it the last time he'd been there.

Evan's stomach growled in response. His cheeks flushed, but he managed a small smile. "That's amazing, Hansen. Thank you."

Having prepped ahead, it didn't take long for Hansen to get their meal ready. Evan sat at the kitchen island and watched him, not saying anything. Hansen left him with his thoughts. He had no doubt Evan needed time after today, and the silence in the room wasn't awkward or heavy. Hansen liked that they could spend time together like this. They didn't need words or explanations. Their silence was filled with unspoken words and shared experiences.

Evan appeared more relaxed by the time they sat down to eat. The air smelled divine, and even though Hansen's day hadn't been as emotionally charged as Evan's, he was starving and happy to keep up the silence for a little while longer. Hansen poured them both a glass of wine, hoping it would help Evan relax even more.

"How are you feeling?" Hansen eventually asked, breaking the silence.

Evan swallowed a bite of pasta. "Better, I think. It's just a little hard to untangle everything right now. But being here with you helps, and I'm glad I could give Davey space."

Hansen reached across the table, taking Evan's hand in his. "You don't have to untangle anything tonight. Just eat, relax, and focus on yourself."

Evan nodded and returned to his meal. He was smiling now, which was good.

After dinner, Hansen cleared the dishes, insisting that Evan relax on the couch. He could feel Evan watching him move around the kitchen, but he didn't mind. It would take them some time to be comfortable together, but this was a good start.

When the kitchen was spotless, Hansen returned to Evan.

He wasn't done taking care of his mate.

"How do you feel about taking a bath?" Hansen offered. "Then we can go to bed or watch TV. Whatever you want."

Evan hesitated for a moment, then nodded. It felt like a step in the right direction for their relationship, but Hansen would do whatever he could to keep him comfortable.

Hansen led Evan to the bathroom upstairs. He wasn't one for baths, so he'd only used it once since he'd moved in. He'd found sitting in the water awkward and boring, but after meeting Evan, he'd bought a few things, just in case Evan enjoyed it more than he did.

He left Evan in his bedroom and went to start the water in the tub. Once the water was warm, he plugged the tub and grabbed the lavender bath bomb he'd bought. He dropped it in, then gathered a bunch of soft towels.

Once Hansen had everything, he inspected the room. Steam rose from the slightly purple water, and the scent of lavender was light in the air. He hoped it would help Evan relax.

"Take your time," Hansen whispered as Evan walked into the bathroom. "I'll be in the bedroom if you need me."

Hansen retreated, leaving Evan alone. He didn't know how

long Evan would be in the bathroom, but he wanted everything to be ready for him when he was done.

He turned on the light on the nightstand instead of the bright overhead light. He opened the bed and cracked the window open so they could get some fresh air. He turned the TV on but kept the volume low.

Evan hadn't brought any clothes with him today, so Hansen grabbed a pair of pajama pants and a t-shirt from his dresser. He couldn't hear anything in the bathroom, so he knocked and waited for Evan to answer.

"Yes?"

Hansen cracked the door open and peeked. "Thought you might need these," he said softly, holding up the folded clothes.

Evan looked up. "Thank you, Hansen." He paused. "For everything."

Hansen smiled, his heart swelling at Evan's vulnerability. "Always, Evan. You deserve every bit of care I can give." And he intended to continue until Evan was sick of him.

He hoped it never happened.

As Hansen turned to leave again, Evan's voice stopped him. "Stay with me," he murmured. "Please."

Hansen hesitated, but he could never say no to his mate. He nodded, sat on the edge of the tub, and reached out to lightly trail his fingers over Evan's shoulder. He was taking a risk, but he didn't think that Evan would push him away. "Tell me what you need."

Evan took a deep breath and looked at Hansen. "I need to feel close to you. Connected. But not...that. Not yet."

Hansen's expression softened, understanding dawning. "Whatever you're ready for."

Evan nodded, his body relaxing further under Hansen's touch. He reached out, his hand finding Hansen's to intertwine their fingers. The connection between them was strong, even without a full bond.

"Kiss me," Evan whispered, his voice barely audible.

Hansen leaned in, his lips brushing against Evan's as gently as he could. The kiss was slow, deliberate, filled with the weight of everything Hansen hadn't yet told Evan. It was a promise of more, a confirmation of their bond, and that he'd take care of Evan until the day he died.

As their lips moved, Evan pulled their linked hands beneath the water. "Closer," he murmured, his body arching toward Hansen.

Hansen was all for that. He knew that Evan would stop him if he did something his mate wasn't ready for, so he didn't hesitate to straighten and get out of his clothes. He heard Evan suck in a breath, but that was it. He didn't tell Hansen to stop, so Hansen carefully lowered himself into the tub behind Evan. The water sloshed gently, enveloping them both. Evan turned his upper body so they could kiss.

"Hansen," he breathed, his voice thick. "Hold me tight."

Hansen complied, wrapping his arms around Evan and squeezing him tightly. The tub wasn't big, but Evan still managed to turn sideways and climb into Hansen's lap, folding his body to fit. He buried his face in Hansen's neck, and Hansen held him.

"Is this okay?" Hansen whispered.

Evan nodded, nuzzling closer. "More than okay. It's perfect."

Their hands roamed, exploring each other's bodies. Hansen traced the lines of Evan's back with his fingertips, eliciting a soft moan from his mate that made him smile.

Evan gasped, his voice trembling. "You feel safe."

Hansen kissed the top of Evan's head, his heart aching with love for this man who had endured so much. He shouldn't have. He should've been protected and cherished. "You're safe with me, Evan."

Evan pulled back slightly, his eyes searching Hansen's. "Can I touch you, too?"

Hansen's breath hitched, his body responding instinctively to Evan's request. "Of course. Take whatever you need from me." Evan might not have yet realized that Hansen was willing to give him anything he asked for, but he would eventually. He'd stop asking and would take him like Hansen wanted him to.

With trembling hands, Evan reached for Hansen to trace his chest. The sensation was electric and intimate. It made Hansen shudder. "You're so strong," Evan murmured, his touch growing bolder. "But so gentle."

Hansen closed his eyes, enjoying the feeling of Evan's hands on his skin. "Not as gentle as you," he replied.

Evan's exploration led him lower, his fingers dancing over Hansen's abdomen before dipping under the water. He glanced up, seeking permission.

"Go ahead," Hansen encouraged, his voice barely above a whisper. "Take control, Evan." It was what he'd missed for years, and Hansen wanted him to have it back.

With a deep breath, Evan slipped his hand under the water to curl his fingers around Hansen's hardened cock. The sensation was intense and caused a rush of heat that made Hansen groan.

"Evan," he breathed, arching his body into the touch. "God, that feels good."

Evan's grip tightened, but his strokes were slow and deliberate. "Does it?" he asked, his voice uncertain.

Hansen nodded, his eyes locked onto Evan's. "Yes, it's perfect."

They stayed like that for what felt like an eternity, their breaths mingling in the steamy air. Hansen cradled Evan's face with his hands, his thumbs brushing over the scars that lingered from his captivity as he gave himself up completely.

"I love you," Hansen whispered, his voice choked with emotion. He should probably wait to say those words, but they felt right. It was what he felt, and he didn't want to keep them from Evan. "Even when you're scared, even when you're unsure, I love you."

Evan's eyes filled with tears. "I love you, too, Hansen. So much."

Their lips met again in a fierce kiss. Hansen slid one hand

under the water, seeking Evan's dick, his touch light as he stroked him in tandem with his own pleasure.

"Harder," Evan panted, his body visibly begging for release. "Please."

Hansen obliged, his strokes firmer, his fingers gliding over Evan's sensitive flesh with ease. "Is this okay?" he asked, his voice hoarse with desire.

"Yes," Evan groaned, his head falling back. "Just like that."

Their moans filled the small bathroom, intermingling with the sound of water sloshing around the tub. Hansen's release came quickly, his body tensing as he spilled into Evan's hand, his breath hitching in his throat. "Evan," he whimpered, the word a prayer on his lips. He'd known he'd love his mate when he met them, but he hadn't expected just how much he would.

Evan's climax followed, his body shaking with the force of it. He clung to Hansen, his fingers digging into Hansen's shoulders as he whimpered. Hansen held him close, wanting him to feel protected and like he could truly let go.

Evan collapsed against Hansen, his breathing still ragged. "Thank you," he whispered.

Hansen held him tightly, his heart full to bursting. "No,

thank *you*, Evan. For trusting me and for letting me in."

They stayed like that for a while, wrapped in each other's arms, ignoring the world outside. It would still be there tomorrow morning.

"Let's get you dried off," Hansen murmured eventually, reluctantly pulling back. "You must be exhausted." And the water was getting cooler. He didn't want Evan to get cold.

Evan nodded. "Yeah, I am. But it was worth it. The whole day was worth it."

Hansen helped him out of the tub, wrapping him in a plush towel before leading him to the bedroom. The bed was already turned down, so Hansen tucked Evan in, his eyes never leaving Evan's.

"Sleep," Hansen whispered, brushing a stray lock of hair from Evan's forehead. "I'll be right here when you wake up." He'd cleaned up the bathroom and got into bed. He didn't want to be away from Evan for too long.

Evan closed his eyes, and Hansen watched him. He could imagine a hundred nights just like this one.

He couldn't wait.

CHAPTER FIVE

Something weird was going on. Evan had first noticed it a few days ago, but it had been easy to dismiss. He had work, Hansen, Davey, and his family. His mother had been calling him every day, and they spent hours talking about what had happened while Evan wasn't home. He'd missed so much that sometimes, it made him want to cry, but when that happened, he reminded himself that he had decades ahead to fix it.

But now that things were settling down, he couldn't ignore the weirdness anymore.

He stared at the flour on the table in front of him. It was

flour, nothing weird to find in a bakery. What *was* weird was the plant in the middle of it.

It hadn't been there before Evan touched the flour. He was supposed to clean it, but as soon as he'd touched it, this fucking thing had sprung from it. Evan didn't know what kind of flour Orion used, but he was pretty sure that it came from this plant. It kind of explained why this plant, in particular, was there, but that was all. Nothing else made sense.

He took a step back, and his feet tangled together. He reached out to grab the table so he wouldn't fall on his face and pressed his hand against the surface. Orion had been baking with oranges, and he'd left the peels and seeds on the table for Evan to clean. Evan's pinky brushed against one of the seeds, and a tiny sprout suddenly burst from it right in front of Evan's eyes.

There was only one explanation. Evan had done it. *He* was the one who'd turned the seed into a plant that was still growing.

He snatched his hand away and cradled it against his chest. The plant stopped growing, but it didn't vanish.

If Evan had to guess, he'd just found out what his mutant

power ability was.

He had no idea what else he could do. He didn't even know what this ability was. Did he make plants grow? Could he grow any plant, anywhere, or did he need a seed or something the plant had been before, like the flour?

"Evan," Orion said.

Evan jumped and squeaked. He turned to glare at Orion, whose head was cocked as he stared at the counter and the tiny orange tree sprouting on it.

"Do I want to know?" Orion asked.

"I don't think you do, but you probably should."

"I'm listening."

"I think I need to stay away from ingredients as much as possible. They seem to grow on me."

"Does that mean you can't pack up pastries anymore?"

Evan bit his lower lip. "I don't know. I think that as long as I don't touch them, I'll be fine."

"Okay. Why don't you go back to the front of the shop? We can talk during lunch break, but in the meantime, it's better if you stay away from my ingredients. I wouldn't want to walk into the kitchen and find a whole orange tree."

Evan glared, but Orion wasn't wrong, so he scurried back

to the front of the shop, happy to forget about his mysterious ability and focus on the job. He served two women and watched as they left the shop. The shop was empty now, which meant he needed something else to distract him.

He grabbed cleaning supplies and went to clean the few tables that had been used since the last time he'd cleaned. Unfortunately, there wasn't much else to do, but as he walked past the potted plant in the corner, he noticed one of the leaves was turning yellow. Without thinking, he grabbed it and pulled.

It turned green again. Evan watched in awe as the leaf turned back to life. He didn't let go, which he realized was a mistake when more leaves started sprouting from the plant.

He swore and stepped back, finally letting go. He stared at the damn thing, sure it was twice as big as it had been before he touched it.

"That's impressive," a voice said from behind him.

He turned to find Matthew, a friend of Hansen and Davey, standing there. The man was staring at the plant, which was still growing, albeit more slowly than it had when Evan was touching it.

"I don't know how to make it stop," Evan confessed.

"I'm pretty sure you just have to wait. It's slowing down."

"I hope so because otherwise, Orion will have to deal with a jungle in his bakery." Which might not be a bad thing. Davey and Hansen were on a raid, which meant that Orion and Evan were jumpy. They were worried, but Evan had been focused on his new ability, while Orion didn't have anything but baking. Maybe creating a problem Orion had to solve would help him not obsess over Davey and what was happening.

"I'm surprised to see you here," he told Matthew as he took another step back from the plant, just in case.

Matthew scowled. "Moore said I was a little too trigger-happy with my electricity. He told me to think about it while I stayed back."

"Hansen mentioned you kept shocking an unconscious hunter."

"The guy was a hunter. Who cares that I was shocking him?"

Evan couldn't say he disagreed. As far as he was concerned, no one should have any pity for hunters. After everything they'd done to him, he certainly didn't.

But he understood why Moore was trying to keep Matthew

under control. Most hunters were evil, but some of them were probably like Orion and Perseus. From what Orion had said, hunting—Evan would call it kidnapping and torturing—supernatural creatures was somewhat of a family tradition for hunters. Sons hunted with their fathers and grandfathers, just like Orion and Perseus had been forced to. They hadn't been able to refuse because they would've been hurt or killed if they had. They'd gotten out, but they'd been lucky. Other hunters might not be, and it wouldn't be fair to hurt them, even though Evan had no doubt they'd hurt people.

"Well, Moore is your boss. If you don't listen to him, he'll put you in timeout," Evan pointed out.

Matthew pouted. He was an adult, but he was short with blond curls and looked completely innocent. It was a stark contrast with the fact that he could fry people to death.

"Are you going to become one of us, then?" Matthew asked.

"What do you mean?"

"Your ability."

Evan glanced at the plant. It had stopped growing, but it *was* about twice as big as it had been before Evan touched it. "I'm not sure how useful that ability would be in a fight. What am I going to do? Hand hunters flowers?"

Matthew hummed as he tapped a fingertip on his chin. "You could make plants grow to trap the hunters like in the movies, you know, with roots and everything. You could wrap branches around the hunters' legs and immobilize them."

Evan couldn't imagine himself doing that. He couldn't imagine himself going on a raid. He was terrified that something would happen to Hansen, and he doubted it would be easier if he was there with his mate. "I think I'll stick with the bakery."

"That's fine. Not all of us who've been changed want to hunt hunters."

"I don't think I can do anything like that."

"No one will ask you to. You can work at the bakery for the rest of your life." Matthew grinned. "In fact, please do. I like it when you give me two cookies for the price of one."

Evan glanced toward the back door. He doubted Orion would be angry, but just in case, he didn't want his boss to hear.

Evan had a soft spot for Matthew, or rather, for the mutants Hansen worked with. He could see how important they were to his mate, and Hansen considered them family, so maybe he spoiled them a bit when they came into the bakery. He wasn't planning on stopping. He wanted them to like him, and if he had to use a little bribery, he would.

Matthew's phone started ringing. He took it out, frowned, and quickly answered. "Hey," he said. "Are you coming back already?"

Evan couldn't hear what the voice on the other side of the phone said, but the tone sounded urgent. Matthew's smile vanished, and his serious expression was more terrifying than imagining him shocking hunters with his ability.

"Yeah, okay. I'll be ready to help if Moore needs me. Yeah, in front of Moore's house."

He hung up and stared at Evan for a moment. Evan wondered if he was going to have to ask. He hoped not.

"The raid went sideways," Matthew explained. "There were more guards and hunters than we expected."

"Hansen? Davey?"

"I don't know, Evan."

*

There was one thing to be said about Hansen's ability — it was helpful to spy on hunters and sneak into labs, but it was less useful when you had to fight a bunch of hunters no one had expected to be there.

He punched a hunter coming at him and ducked when another tried to stab him. He turned to face the second hunter, but Teddy was already there, exploding the hunter's hand with his ability. The man screamed and clutched his arm to his chest as he stumbled back.

Hansen grimaced. "Was that really necessary?"

Teddy gave him an unimpressed look. "Would you have preferred getting stabbed?"

"It's messy."

"You're jealous you can't explode things."

Hansen grinned. "I am."

Teddy smiled back, but it didn't last long. They both turned toward more hunters coming. Hansen wondered if they were ever going to end.

He didn't know what had happened, but the people in the facility they were in had expected them to attack. Maybe they'd heard about other labs the mutants had raided, or maybe they were protecting something big they did here. Either way, between the guards and the hunters, the mutants were in trouble.

It was a good thing they had tricks up their sleeves. If they hadn't been mutants, they would've been defeated. As it was, they were holding their own, and if Hansen wasn't mistaken, the tide was turning in their favor. It was just happening a little too slowly for him to be comfortable with.

He grimaced when a hunter mummified in front of his eyes. Davey used the water he'd stolen from the hunter's body and wrapped it around a guard's head, causing him to claw at his face to try to breathe. Hansen turned away. He'd seen this scene several times before, and it was never easy to deal with. It was necessary, but it didn't mean he wanted to watch.

His ability wasn't going to help him in this situation, and while he was doing a good enough job in his human form, he'd have an easier time if he shifted. He didn't usually shift on raids because it made communicating with the others more complicated, but he felt that today was a good day to do so. It would be easier for him to defend his fellow mutants and himself if he had claws and fangs.

He kicked a hunter in the back of the knee as he walked past, headed for the corner of the room. He needed a few seconds to shift, and he didn't want any of the hunters to attack him while he did so.

Olga nodded at him and punched a hunter. Thankfully, the man didn't get back to his feet after he slumped to the floor, so Hansen had plenty of time to let his lion out.

He didn't bother taking his clothes off. He was wearing one of the uniforms they wore on raids, so it wasn't like he'd miss them. Well, he probably would once he needed to shift back, but that could be easily dealt with. In the meantime, he'd put his lion to work.

He roared as soon as he was shifted. He saw a few of the hunters jump and grinned, pleased when one of them whimpered and lost control of his bladder. That one wasn't going to last long. Frankly, it was a small miracle that he was still here and hadn't run away screaming as soon as he'd seen the mutants.

Hansen snapped his teeth at the hunter, who screamed and turned to run. Hansen disliked letting any of the hunters escape, but it would be better if he focused on the ones still fighting.

He caught a guard by the calf and pulled him away from Elsa. The man screamed as Hansen's fangs sank into his flesh.

Hansen disliked the taste of blood, but it was still satisfying to know that he was fighting hunters and avenging his mate.

There was no way to know if any of the hunters and the guards here had ever hurt Evan, but Hansen had decided that they might as well have. These people were all the same. They sacrificed human lives for money and their own interests, and that was enough for him to despise every single one of them.

Hansen lost count of how many hunters he dealt with. He worked his way through the room, helping the other mutants who needed it. He didn't realize that meant he got separated from his group until he found himself stepping into a side room.

The room was lined with cages, most of them occupied. He desperately wanted to free the people inside, but he couldn't do it now. They needed to take care of the hunters before they could help anyone because freeing them with so many hunters around would be dangerous.

Hansen forced himself to ignore the cries for help and turned to return to the main room when his gaze stopped on a guard. The man was standing in the middle of the hallway between the cages and pointing his gun at Hansen. He smelled like fear.

Hansen slowly faced the guard. He was wearing a uniform, like the others, but he was sweating, and there was a long gash on his arm that had cut through his shirt. He was bleeding, but he held the gun steadily. Hansen was pretty sure that if he tried jumping the guy, he'd get shot, and if that happened, Evan wouldn't be happy.

He stayed as still as he could, wondering what he should do. He couldn't talk the guard down in this form, and while he wasn't looking forward to being naked as he tried to reason with man, it would be better than growling at him.

Hansen shifted back to his human form. He stood tall, not caring about his nakedness. He noticed the guard's eyes widen, and the man quickly looked over Hansen's shoulder.

"What are you doing?" the guard asked.

Hansen raised his hands. "I just want to talk to you."

"There's nothing to talk about. You're going to help me escape."

"You could escape on your own right now. Everyone is busy fighting. They won't notice you sneaking away."

"I'm not going to risk it." The man waved his gun. "If I take you hostage, they'll be forced to let me go."

"Do you really think that's the best idea?"

An explosion made both of them jump. From the sound of it, it hadn't been very big, but it had been close. Hansen hoped that Teddy had caused it. He didn't want to have to deal with explosions not caused by their side. They never ended well for anyone, not even the hunters.

Hansen moved toward the guard, only to find himself facing the gun again.

"Stop moving," the guard snapped.

"I'm not going to stop you from leaving," Hansen tried to reassure the guard. He knew how to deal with hunters, but guards were always a little more complicated. He was sure that some of them had taken the job without knowing what they'd have to deal with. They'd probably been horrified, but they'd stayed. They'd gotten paid to guard shifters and humans who were being hurt by their bosses.

Something moved behind the guard, but he didn't notice. Hansen did his best not to look in the direction so he wouldn't draw the guard's attention. He sucked in a breath when that something moved closer and revealed itself to be another guard. He was wearing the same uniform and had a gun in his hand, too.

Shit. Hansen really was in trouble.

The first guard started to turn when he realized there was someone there with them. Hansen didn't know what to expect, but it wasn't for the second guard to raise his gun and hit the first guard in the face with it.

Someone in one of the cages whimpered, but Hansen kept his focus on the second guard. He was looking down at the first guard, who was unconscious on the floor. The guard didn't stay still for long, though. He quickly put his gun away, then grabbed the first guard's arms and dragged him toward one of the cages. He hesitated, but instead of opening the cage, he grabbed handcuffs from the guard's belt and used them to tie the man to the cage. He pulled on the handcuffs to be sure they wouldn't open, then finally turned to face Hansen.

"I think you should either shift back or find some clothes," he said.

"I'll shift back. Why did you do it?"

"Because the only reason I'm here is to find my siblings."

Hansen supposed that was as good a reason as any other.

*

"What do you mean, you don't know?" Evan asked Matthew.

"Exactly what I said. I don't know what's going on."

"You just got a call that explained it to you."

Matthew shook his head. "I got a call from Olga telling me that things had gone sideways and that I needed to be ready to get picked up if they needed me."

"Well? *Are* you ready to get picked up?"

"I need to go to Moore's house. That's where they'll pick me up."

"Let's go, then."

Matthew was already shaking his head again. "You can't come with me."

Evan had never threatened anyone seriously. Today, though, he put his hands on his hips and glared at Matthew. "You know that thing you told me to do with roots?"

"The one where I thought you could immobilize hunters by using your ability with plants?"

"That one. Do you want me to use it on you?"

"I know you want to help, but getting yourself hurt and putting yourself in danger isn't going to do anything. Hansen is just going to be even more worried if he finds out you're there."

"I need to do *something*."

Evan understood that he'd be a liability if he went. He

couldn't fight, and he had no idea how he'd react if he was forced to enter a lab again. That didn't mean he was willing to stay at the bakery and stare at the wall while his mate was in danger.

"As long as that something isn't putting yourself in danger, I think we can compromise."

Evan wouldn't have taken no for an answer, but he was glad he wouldn't have to fight Matthew. He quickly took his apron off and threw it onto the counter, only to stop moving when he remembered that Orion didn't know that something was wrong. "We have to tell Orion. Davey is in that lab, too."

Matthew grimaced. "Olga and Moore are going to kick my ass when they find out about this."

"Do I look like I care?" Evan snapped. He liked Matthew, but if he had to choose between him and Hansen, he wouldn't hesitate. He needed to know that Hansen was okay, and the only way to do that was to stick with Matthew.

He glared at the man and hoped that Matthew wouldn't take the opportunity to leave while he talked to Orion. Even if he did, Evan would find him. He knew where Matthew was going.

Evan burst into the back room, making Orion jump. He

was working at one of the long tables and turned to frown at Evan. There was a spot of flour on his cheek, and his hands were dirty, but when he saw Evan's expression, he grabbed a towel. "What happened?"

"The raid went sideways."

"Davey?"

Evan shook his head. "I don't know anything else, but Matthew is here, and he's supposed to go to Moore's house in case they need to pick him up to help with the fight. I'm going with him."

"I'm coming, too," Orion said, already reaching for the oven.

He and Evan quickly worked together to turn off everything that needed to be turned off. Orion didn't need to come back to a burned-out bakery.

It only took a handful of minutes, but Evan was relieved to see that Matthew was still waiting for them when they walked through the door to the front of the shop. He was on his phone, typing something, but he quickly put it away when he heard them.

"Come on. I don't want to waste time."

Evan wasn't offended. He didn't want to waste time,

either.

They didn't run through the streets of the village so they wouldn't alarm anyone, but it was a close thing. Evan wanted to scream at the people going about their day as if nothing was happening. How could they not be worried about the people who'd saved them?

He swallowed and told himself to stop being a dick. These people didn't know what was happening. They probably had no idea that the mutants were out on a raid. They'd been freed, and they deserved to live their lives without fear, which was what they were doing.

The door of Moore's house flew open as soon as they reached it. Moore's mate, Jolyn, waved at them to come in. "Rikar's already here," he said as he led them through the house.

Evan had heard about Moore's mate, but he'd never met him before. He looked like he couldn't hurt a fly, but his expression was fierce, as if he was ready to find his mate and kick ass to save him. Evan felt the same, even though he and Hansen weren't bonded yet.

They would be. After today, there was no way Evan would allow Hansen anywhere without him if they weren't bonded.

He needed to know if Hansen was in trouble. He needed to be able to feel that something was happening to his mate. If it hadn't been for Matthew, he would still be at the bakery, working as if everything was fine.

They walked out the back door in the kitchen. Evan had no idea where they were going or what was happening, but he didn't care because Matthew seemed to be on board with it.

As Jolyn had said, Rikar was already there. He was pacing the space between the backyard and the forest. He looked up when he heard them, nodded at Matthew, then cocked his head as he watched Evan.

"You can't go with Matthew," he warned.

"I can do whatever I want," Evan snapped. He wouldn't let anyone keep him from his mate.

Orion grabbed Evan's shoulder and squeezed. "Calm down."

"How can I calm down? Hansen is in trouble, and I can't do anything to help him. What am I supposed to do? Get back to work? Stare at the sky and pray?"

"You need to breathe. Come on, Evan. Hansen wouldn't want you to freak out, especially when you don't know what's going on."

"I'm freaking out *because* I don't know what's going on. If I knew what Hansen was doing, I wouldn't be."

"I don't know either," Rikar explained. "I got a call from Moore, so I know something's happened, but he didn't give me details. Matthew?"

"Olga called me. She said to be ready to get picked up, just in case."

"People can't shimmer in the village," Evan pointed out.

Rikar shook his head. "That's not exactly true. There are designated spots, including this one."

Evan frowned and looked around. He couldn't see anything different, but they wouldn't be here if Rikar was lying.

"We didn't want the villagers to be alarmed at people shimmering in and out during raids, so we designated a few spots in the village to be private shimmering areas," Rikar explained. "This spot is one of those. Now, we just need to wait."

Evan raked a hand through his hair. "How can we do that? We don't know what's going on. We don't know if someone was hurt. How do you expect me to wait until someone comes back?"

145

"We don't have a choice," Orion murmured. "I know how hard it is. It's not the first time Davey's been on a raid, and I have to stay back. They'll be fine, though."

Evan wrapped his arms around himself. "You can't know that. You can't know anything for sure. Hansen could be hurt, or worse, and I wouldn't know."

"Davey is fine," Orion offered.

Davey and Orion were bonded, which meant that Orion could feel Davey. He'd be panicking if something had happened to Davey, and strangely, knowing that did help Evan relax.

But he couldn't help but wonder about Hansen. If something happened to him, Evan wouldn't know. He wouldn't be able to feel it. He'd still be here, waiting and hoping.

How was Evan supposed to deal with that knowledge?

He looked down at his feet. He'd been relieved to find out that his ability would be useless to hurt people, but now, he wished things were different. He *wanted* to hurt people. He wanted to hurt the hunters who were attacking his mate.

But the only thing he could do was wait.

*

Hansen didn't stray far from his new friend, the guard. He had no idea why the man was helping him and the other mutants beyond what the guard had said, but he didn't trust him. Maybe the guard *was* here to find his siblings, but Hansen had no way of knowing who these siblings were and why they could be there.

He'd assumed they'd be in a cage, but he might be wrong. Maybe this guy's siblings were doctors. Maybe they worked in this facility. Maybe the guard was lying. Whatever was happening, Hansen would make sure the man didn't hurt anyone.

"This would be easier if we could talk," the guard said as he stepped over a fallen hunter. He'd taken his gun out again, but he hadn't used it yet.

He showed the guard his teeth. He wasn't trying to be intimidating—okay, maybe he was trying to be a *bit* intimidating—but he wanted the guard to know he was listening.

The man didn't look impressed. "Yeah, I can do that, too." He grinned at Hansen. It wasn't a nice smile. "But I get it. You don't trust me. I'm a shifter, too, just so you know."

Hansen pressed his nose against the man's leg, only for the man to push him away.

"I'm wearing one of those sprays, just in case. I didn't want anyone to realize I was a shifter. You know what they do to us in this place."

Hansen did, so he understood why the man would have used one of those sprays, but he still had dozens of questions. He couldn't ask them in this form, but he would as soon as the fight was over.

Hansen noticed Olga fighting with two hunters. When she punched one of them so hard that he stumbled back and hit Hansen's side, Hansen twisted his upper body and grabbed the man's wrist. The man screamed, so Hansen gave him a good shake. Blood spurted in his mouth, so as soon as he dropped the hunter's wrist, he spluttered and rubbed his muzzle with his paw.

"Aren't you wishing that you could shoot them instead of biting them?" the guard asked as he raised his gun. Hansen glared at him. The guard didn't seem intimidated because he grinned and added, "I'm Franklin."

Hansen hadn't expected to get a name, and he couldn't give one back, so he just blinked. Franklin rolled his eyes and turned. Hansen watched as he shot one of the hunters who had been fighting Davey.

Impressive.

As much as Hansen wanted to focus on Franklin, he couldn't. He tried to stay as close to the man as he could as they fought, but he lost sight of him a few times. He half expected Franklin to be gone by the time the last hunter fell to the floor, screaming, but the man was still there.

It was as if everyone still standing in the room turned to Franklin. He quickly raised his hands and dropped his gun, kicking it away so he couldn't pick it up again.

"I know you can't smell it, but I'm a shifter. I'm here because I'm looking for my siblings."

Hansen hoped he wasn't lying because if he was, it wouldn't end well for him.

Hansen shifted back. No one said anything about his state of nudity, and while he didn't care, he also didn't want to drag unconscious hunters around with his dick flopping around. He crouched next to one of the doctors, who was watching him with wide eyes, and forced the man to give up his white coat. He slid it on, closing all the buttons before looking down at himself to make sure everything important was covered.

"You have nice legs," Franklin said.

Hansen glared at him again. "And you have a big mouth that you can't seem to keep closed."

"My mother always said that."

"She was right."

Franklin's expression turned wistful. "She was, wasn't she?"

From the way he was talking about her, it was clear that she wasn't in his life anymore. Hansen wanted to ask if she'd died or if something had happened to her, but it was none of his business.

"Hansen?" Moore asked as he stepped between the fallen hunters.

Right. Hansen was chatting with a guard. Everyone was staring at him because they didn't understand what was happening.

"This is Franklin. He says he's a shifter and that he's here to find his siblings."

Moore looked Franklin up and down. "Do we believe him?"

"I don't know. He took out a guard who was threatening

me with a gun and wanted to take me hostage, and he helped me take down a few more hunters, so I guess I'd give him the benefit of the doubt."

"Does that mean I can go?" Franklin asked.

Moore arched a brow. "So eager to get away from us."

"Because neither of my siblings is in the cages I found."

"You could probably use some help to find them. Why don't you stick around for a bit?"

Franklin looked like he wanted to argue, but he glanced around the room and seemed to think better of it. If he was lying, it wouldn't do him any good to try and run. Considering the dozens of people standing there, poking at fallen hunters and dragging them into piles, he could probably tell how that would end. And if he *was* telling the truth, he'd want more people to help him find his siblings.

The only option he had was to stay.

"Any survivors?" Moore asked as he turned his attention to the rest of the room.

Hansen leaned against the wall and watched. Most of the hunters were dead, which hopefully meant the other hunters would stop supplying the labs with people for a while. Hansen had no idea how many hunters were out there, but from the little he'd learned from Orion, he knew they weren't as organized as they seemed from the outside. Hansen hoped that what had happened today had given their organization a massive blow.

And not only because they'd tried to kill him.

"You're not going to help?" Franklin said as he leaned next to Hansen.

"I can't."

"I'm not going to run if that's what you're afraid of."

Hansen eyed him. "How am I supposed to trust you? You don't smell like a shifter, and you're wearing a guard's uniform. As far as I know, you lied to me to save your ass."

Franklin nodded. He didn't look offended by what Hansen had just said. "You're not wrong."

"I know I'm not. I'm going to keep an eye on you, Franklin."

"I'm not planning on sticking around."

"Whatever you were planning, it's going to have to change. There's no way Moore's gonna let you leave."

Franklin opened his mouth, possibly to argue, but Moore beat him to it. "Hansen's right. I'm not letting you go."

"I already told you that I was here to find my siblings."

152

"It could be a lie."

"Or maybe your siblings are doctors," Hansen offered.

"They're not doctors," Franklin snapped. "They were taken, and I know they're in one of the labs. I need to find them."

"If you're telling the truth, we'll help you," Moore offered. "It's kind of our specialty. If you're lying, though, you're in trouble."

Franklin shook his head. "I'm not lying. I never wanted to hurt anyone."

"Yet you shot several people today."

"Hunters. I shot hunters."

The way Franklin spat out the last word told Hansen everything he needed to know about how Franklin felt. He believed the guy. He wasn't sure what would come out of it, but it was clear that Franklin despised the hunters and probably wanted all of them dead. It made sense if he was telling the truth and his siblings had been taken by hunters. Of course he'd want all hunters dead. Hansen did, too, with only a few exceptions.

"Hansen, shimmer back to the village," Moore said, turning his attention back to Hansen. "You need clothes. I want you to take the wounded with you, along with Franklin."

"What village?" Franklin asked.

"The village where we live. I'd like to talk to you about your siblings and what you were doing here today, if that's okay with you."

Franklin hesitated. "I bet that if I say it's not, you won't be happy."

Moore smirked. "Our village has a small jail. You can choose between ending up behind bars and talking to me."

Franklin sighed. "Fine. I'll talk to you."

"Good. Now help Hansen."

Teddy, Elsa, and Leon were working on the worst of the wounded. As soon as they were stable, Elsa and Teddy would start shimmering them back to the village, and it looked like Franklin and Hansen would go along for the ride.

Hansen turned to Franklin. "It won't be long."

"I'm fine waiting. My siblings aren't here, anyway," Franklin answered.

Hansen could only imagine what the man was going through. If he'd really lost his siblings to the labs, he had to be in hell. It sounded like he'd been looking for them for a while and had probably visited several labs.

He still hadn't found them.

CHAPTER SIX

E van was going nuts. He should be out there, helping his mate. He should be able to feel what Hansen was going through. At the very least, he should be trying to find a way to get to Hansen.

He stopped pacing for a moment to glare at Rikar, who seemed amused but didn't move from his spot where he was leaning against the railing of the porch steps. He already knew what Evan wanted, but he wasn't going to give it to him. Evan had tried to convince him, had even begged, yet here they were.

"I need to get to Hansen," Evan tried again. "What if it was *your* mate?"

"It was, once. Now that we have a daughter, Hayes doesn't go on raids anymore, but he used to."

"So you understand why I have to go."

"I understand why this is difficult for you, but I would never have dreamed of going on a raid with Hayes."

"Then you're a bad mate," Evan snapped. He sucked in a breath and rubbed his eyes. "I'm sorry. I didn't mean that." It wouldn't do him any good to make an enemy out of the leader of the tribe he lived with.

Rikar pushed away from the stairs to grab Evan's shoulder. "It's fine. You don't have to worry about me kicking you out just because you disagree with me."

Evan sucked in a breath, then another. He glanced at Orion, who was sitting on the porch steps and bouncing his knee. He stared straight ahead as if Davey were about to appear in the middle of the yard.

Maybe he was. That *was* what they were waiting for, even though so far, nothing had happened.

Evan turned to Matthew, who was still on his phone. "Any news?"

"No. I haven't heard anything else from Olga. At this point,

I don't think they're picking me up."

"Which means they don't need you."

Matthew slowly nodded. "In theory."

"What do you mean, in theory?"

"Well, they might have managed to win the fight without my help, which is what I hope happened, but maybe all of them are incapacitated and can't come."

Evan heard Orion mutter, "Was that really necessary?"

That was it. It was all Evan could take.

Something in him snapped. For a moment, he didn't understand what it was. He was angry and terrified, and he needed Hansen. Someone made a strangled noise, and Evan saw that roots had shot out of the earth and grabbed Rikar's legs.

Rikar didn't seem to be worried. He poked at one of the roots that was inching toward his upper body as if it were the most interesting thing he'd ever seen. The root wiggled, almost like a happy dog.

"You're the one doing this?" Rikar asked, looking at Evan.

"He is, and he needs to stop," Matthew said. "Breathe, Evan."

"I don't know what's happening," Evan complained. "I'm

not doing it on purpose. It's never happened before, and I don't know how to stop it."

"It's the same thing that you did at the bakery. Your ability is coming out."

Evan understood that, but between everything, he wasn't sure he could get it under control. The problem was that he *had* to find a way because the roots were crawling up Rikar's body. Several had twined around his arms, and if Evan wasn't mistaken, they were trying to immobilize him. When one touched Rikar's throat, Evan squeezed his eyes shut. "No," he told himself. "I'm not going to hurt anyone with this ability. I don't care what it is or how it works."

He tried to keep himself under control, but it felt like going down a slippery road. It was like water in his hands. No matter how hard he tried to keep it—whatever it was—there, he couldn't. It was necessary, but he was unable to stop.

Orion grabbed Evan's shoulders, causing him to open his eyes. "Breathe," he ordered.

Evan nodded and tried to do just that. He sucked in a breath, then another. It became easier to breathe, but as soon as he turned toward Rikar, he started panicking again. The roots were extending. Rikar still didn't look alarmed, which

Evan didn't understand, but it was good that at least one person wasn't panicking.

"This is why we told you it would be a bad idea for you to go find Hansen," Matthew said. "You don't have control over yourself or your ability."

"You're not helping," Orion told him.

"I don't think anything is going to help. This is something that Evan has to do by himself."

"And he's not going to be able to do it if you berate him."

"I'm not berating him. I'm just pointing out the obvious."

Evan was going to yell at them as soon as this mess was over. Was now really the time to bicker?

"You're doing a good job, Evan," Rikar said in a calm voice. "I don't know what it's like to have your ability, but if it's anything like Hayes's ability to fly, freaking out is the last thing you want to do."

"Hayes can fly?"

"It's how we met. He crashed through my roof."

Evan laughed. He'd seen Hayes around, and he seemed like a nice guy. They hadn't talked, but Evan knew that Hayes was close to a lot of the mutants. He'd thought Hayes had gone on the raid, but after what Rikar had said, he suspected that Hayes was at home with their daughter.

As he should be. If Rikar and Hayes had a daughter, it made sense that Hayes hadn't gone on the raid. Evan wished the same could be said for Hansen. Instead, his mate was in danger, and Evan didn't know what was happening to him.

"You're losing focus again," Orion said, his voice snapping Evan out of his thoughts. "Come on, Evan. I know you can do it."

"*I* don't even know if I can do it," Evan said, glancing at Rikar only to find that he was encased in roots up to his neck. Branches from the closest tree were also reaching for him, almost as if they wanted to pull him into the woods. It reminded Evan of a fantasy movie. It was creepy.

He was creepy. When he'd heard about the mutants having abilities, he'd hoped he wouldn't get one. He'd known there was a good chance that he would, though, and when he'd realized that it had to do with plants, he'd been relieved. He couldn't hurt anyone with plants, right?

Wrong.

"What the hell is going on here?"

Evan snapped his face in the direction from which the voice had come. His eyes widened at the sight of Hansen standing there, wearing a doctor's white coat that left his legs and feet bare. He was standing next to Teddy, whose brows had shot up his forehead, and a bunch of other people who'd seen better days.

They weren't who Evan focused on. He should probably feel guilty about that since they were clearly hurt, while Hansen didn't seem to be, but all of his thoughts were on his mate.

Hansen was home. He was there, in front of Evan, whole and seemingly healthy.

Their bond sang between them as Evan took a step forward. Orion quickly stepped aside to let him pass, and as soon as he was free of interference, Evan ran forward.

Hansen smiled and opened his arms. Evan wished he could say that it was like a scene in a movie in which he threw himself into his mate's arms, and they kissed and promised each other they would never be apart again. Instead, he tripped and almost fell on his face.

Luckily for him, Hansen wasn't far. He lunged forward and grabbed Evan's arm, pulling him forward. He looked at Evan with a frown, but Evan didn't give him time to ask if he was okay. He wrapped his arms around Hansen's neck and squeezed tightly, making Hansen squeak.

"Evan?" Hansen asked as he hugged Evan's waist.

"You were in danger, and I didn't know. You could've died, and I would've had no clue. I would have gone ahead with my life until someone came to find me and tell me something happened to you."

"I'm fine," Hansen promised.

Evan tilted his head up to glare at him. "This time. What about the next time there are more hunters than you expected? What about when one of the people in the cages attacks you, or when the guards fight back?"

"I understand why you're scared, but the only solution I can think of is for me to stop going on raids, and I'm not sure I'm ready to do that."

"Or we could bond. If we did, I would feel you. I would know if you were okay." And Evan couldn't think of a better reason to bond with his mate. He already knew he loved Hansen. He didn't need a bond to be sure of that. No, he needed the bond to be sure that Hansen was okay.

*

Hansen had no idea what was happening beyond the fact that

Evan was freaking out.

"You want us to bond?" he asked.

Evan clung more tightly to Hansen. "Yes. We can do it right now."

Hansen cupped the back of Evan's head with a hand. "There's no need for that. I'm fine, and I'm not going anywhere."

"Are you saying you don't want to bond with me?"

"I'm saying I don't want to bond with you here in front of all these people."

Evan stared for a moment longer before nodding. Hansen expected him to step away, but instead, he buried his face against Hansen's chest.

Hansen hadn't expected Evan to be here when he arrived. He shouldn't have been. Evan wasn't supposed to know that something had happened during the raid. He was supposed to be at the bakery, helping Orion and selling pastries.

Instead, both he and Orion were here. In fact, Orion had been standing in front of Evan when Hansen had arrived, his hands raised as if he was trying to control him. It didn't make sense.

What made even less sense was whatever was happening

with Rikar.

He was standing there, looking entirely at ease, even though his body was encased in what looked like roots. Hansen knew what he was seeing, but part of him wondered if he was dreaming. Maybe he'd been hit upside the head during the raid?

He held Evan close as he stared. Those were definitely roots. They came from the ground and wrapped around Rikar's legs and body up to his neck. If Hansen wasn't mistaken, though, the roots were slithering back into the ground. They were slow-moving, but they *were* moving, and soon enough, Rikar's shoulders and upper chest were free.

"What the hell happened here?" Hansen asked.

"Your mate happened," Matthew answered. "What about the raid? Olga called me, but no one came to pick me up. Unless that's why you're here?"

Hansen shook his head. He tried stepping away from Evan, but Evan clung to him harder. Hansen didn't have it in him to make his mate cry or worry more than he already was, so he decided they could continue hugging as he explained. "Things weren't great for a while, but we managed. We're starting to shimmer back the people who need medical attention."

"Thank God," Matthew said, his shoulders relaxed. "I'll call the healers."

"Yeah, you probably should. These are the worst ones, but there will be more people coming. We also have a bunch of hunters to stick in jail."

"I'll call Olga or Moore and see what they want me to do."

"Davey?" Orion asked, looking like he might start crying if Hansen had bad news for him.

"The last time I saw him, he was poking at one of the doctors from the facility. He's fine."

Orion's shoulders slumped. "Thank you."

"I didn't do anything. He kept himself safe."

"Thank you for telling me. I can feel he's all right, but I'm not used to any of this."

Orion could feel that Davey was fine because they'd bonded. Evan, on the other hand, had no idea how Hansen was because the bond between them wasn't complete yet. That was why he'd mentioned bonding as soon as Hansen had arrived. It was why he'd wanted to do it right away. He was afraid he'd lose Hansen and wouldn't know that something had happened to him.

Hansen's heart broke a bit. He never wanted his mate to worry, but considering what he did for a living, it would happen. Hell, Evan would probably worry about him even if he went to the grocery store. He'd lost so much in his life, and while Hansen thought that he was strong enough to survive losing a lot more, he didn't want his mate to have to go through anything else. He wanted to give Evan everything he could want, including the bond between them.

"Davey was great, like always," Hansen reassured Orion. "I saw him drown at least one hunter."

Orion blinked as if he didn't know what to make of that. Hansen wasn't sure what to make of it, either. It never got any less weird.

"So, is anyone going to tell me what's up with Rikar?" he asked.

The roots had finally retreated back into the ground. Rikar was stretching his arms and poking at the ground with his toes. Maybe he was trying to get the roots to come out again. Hansen didn't understand why anyone would want that, but Rikar had always been a little strange.

"That would be me," Evan muttered before finally leaning away. He didn't let go of Hansen, though. He clung to him like a barnacle, and Hansen was pretty sure that if he could get away with it, Evan would climb into his arms.

"You?" Hansen asked because he didn't understand.

"I figured out what my ability is."

It took Hansen a moment to understand what Evan was saying. "Roots?"

Evan waved his hand. "Plants in general. Just ask the potted plant at the bakery. The place is going to become a jungle if I'm allowed to touch it."

Evan's voice was light, even though there was a hint of nervousness in his tone. Hansen knew how afraid Evan had been that his ability would hurt people, so he was glad to find out that wouldn't be the case. Sure, Evan could still hurt someone while controlling plants, but it would be much easier to deal with than Teddy's ability, for example. Evan would've been crushed if he'd been able to make people explode.

Hansen kissed Evan's cheek. "Plants, huh?"

"I guess. It could've been worse."

"So you're fine with it?"

Evan grimaced. "I wouldn't say that. I can only accept it, right? There's no way for me to turn off this ability. Trust me.

I tried."

Hansen never wanted Evan to feel like he was wrong or like he should do something different. He'd had no say in this new ability or in the way it was forced into him. None of them had. The only thing all of the mutants could do was accept what had been done to them and that they were different now. It was easier for some and harder for others, but in the end, whatever had been done to them in those labs had made them the people they were today.

Hansen couldn't regret what had been done to him because if he didn't have the ability to cloak himself, he wouldn't be raiding labs and saving people. Evan wouldn't be the person he was now if he hadn't gone through everything he'd gone through. Hansen wished he hadn't, but there was no changing the past. He was happy to have Evan in any way he could get him.

He hoped that Evan would be able to accept his ability. Whether or not he could, Hansen would be there, helping him to control it and maybe even use it.

He pressed his lips against Evan's. "You'll be fine. I'll help."

Matthew cleared his throat. "That's great and all, but

maybe you could help us get these people to the healers?"

Evan squeezed Hansen harder and glared over Hansen's shoulder at Matthew. "Can't *you* do that? Hansen needs to find some clothes. I'm not letting him run around half-naked."

Matthew barked out a laugh. "What if he *wants* to run around half-naked?"

"I don't want to, so Evan's right. I need clothes before I can help you with anything." Hansen turned. "Have you called Olga or Moore?"

Matthew nodded as he helped one of the mutants to her feet. "They don't need us back at the facility. They'll take care of gathering everyone who needs to be brought here and of the facility once it's empty."

They would set it on fire. It was what they always did because that way, no one could use anything inside the building again. It wouldn't stop the people setting up in the labs, but hopefully, it would slow them down.

"What can I do?" Franklin asked.

Hansen turned to tell him that he had no idea because Moore hadn't ordered him to do anything about Franklin, but before he could open his mouth, roots shot out of the ground and wrapped around the man.

When Rikar had been wrapped up in the roots, he'd looked amused and interested. Now that it was Franklin's turn, the man appeared alarmed and scared. Hansen didn't blame him. Even though he knew that Evan was doing this, he was a little scared, too.

*

Evan couldn't breathe. What was this man doing here? How had he survived the raid? He wasn't tied up. He wasn't even wounded. He was walking around as if his presence here was normal, wearing a guard's uniform.

"Evan?" Hansen asked.

His tone made it obvious that he was afraid Evan would snap. Evan couldn't blame him because it felt like he already had. He didn't have any control over the roots that were winding their way around the guard's body. He just wanted the man to disappear, and apparently, the roots were already working on it.

Things got even more alarming when the ground under the guard started splitting. Evan was pretty sure that if he didn't stop, the ground would swallow the guard whole.

Wouldn't that be a sight?

"Evan?" Hansen tried again.

Evan blinked. "He's a guard."

"I know. He wouldn't be here if we weren't sure he wouldn't hurt anyone. Moore agreed to his presence at the village. In fact, he demanded it."

Evan still didn't understand. "He's a *guard*. He was at one of the facilities where I was kept at. I saw him."

Hansen frowned and looked at the guard. "Is that true?"

The guard's eyes were wide, and he was trying to push away the roots, but they weren't leaving. They couldn't because Evan was controlling them.

"I already told you that I was looking for my siblings. I worked at several facilities. I don't know you, man. I've seen hundreds of people in cages."

"And you did nothing to free any of them?" Evan asked.

"I couldn't. If I had, they would have known it was me, and I would've had to stop looking for my brother and my sister. Please. You know what happens in those labs. You were there, too. You know what they're doing to my siblings and why I have to find them."

Could Evan believe this man? He'd been a guard, but he

hadn't been one of the bad ones. He hadn't helped Evan escape, but he also hadn't hurt him.

Normally, Evan wouldn't forgive the man. He was saying that he'd been looking for his siblings, though, and if they were in one of the facilities, Evan knew precisely what they were going through. He couldn't blame this man for doing everything he could for his family.

He still wanted to hurt him.

A hand squeezed Evan's shoulder hard. "Please," Hansen said. "Franklin saved my life. One of the hunters was going to take me as a hostage, but Franklin knocked him out."

That was the only thing that could convince Evan to let go. The problem was that he didn't know how to do it. "I can't control it."

"What do you mean, you can't control it?" Franklin asked as a root wrapped around his throat.

Evan squeezed his eyes shut and took a deep breath. "*This is what happens in those labs. They turn you into something you don't recognize and don't know how to control.*"

"I'm sorry that happened to you, but my brother and my sister need me. Please don't kill me."

Lips suddenly landed on Evans, shocking him. He didn't

have to open his eyes to know who was kissing him. He could feel it in the bond that vibrated between him and Hansen. The bond wanted more, as did Evan.

"Is this going to keep happening?" Matthew asked.

Evan blinked and leaned away from Hansen. He wasn't surprised to see that Franklin was free. He also wasn't surprised when Franklin took a step away from him when he saw that Evan was watching him.

"I don't know," he told Matthew. "I really didn't mean any of this."

"He's going to have to learn control," Rikar said. "And maybe try not to get angry. It's clear that this ability is reactive to your feelings. You were angry at me because I wouldn't let you go after Hansen, and at Franklin because you thought he was here to hurt you and the people you care about."

It was true. It seemed like Evan's ability got out of control when Evan himself did. It wasn't the same as it had been at the bakery when he'd touched the potted plant. That plant had grown out of his control, too, but not like this. He hadn't been afraid that the plant would hurt someone.

He was afraid that the roots would, that *he* would since he was the one controlling them.

174

"I'm a shifter," Franklin explained.

He was keeping some distance between himself and Evan, but Evan didn't think it mattered. If his ability wanted Franklin, it could reach him.

"Or so you say," Hansen said.

Franklin narrowed his eyes at him. "I *am* a shifter, and you'll realize that as soon as the spray fades or you let me shower. I worked as a guard in the facilities to find my siblings. They were kidnapped, and my mother was killed. I've been looking for them since then."

Evan wasn't a hundred percent sure he believed Franklin, but if Franklin was telling the truth, Evan felt sorry for him. "What are their names?"

"Leah and Garrett. They're twins."

Evan chewed on his lower lip as he tried to remember if he'd ever talked to a Leah or a Garrett. Initially, he'd talked to as many people as he could in the cages, hoping to find solidarity and help. He'd realized soon enough that most of the people who were locked up had lost hope. It wasn't that they didn't care what was done to them. It was that they didn't think they could ever escape the labs and had lost the will to try.

Evan never had. Evan had always known that Davey was out there, looking for him. Maybe that was what had made the difference. Davey knew what he was looking for. He knew about the labs and how dangerous they were. The other prisoners hadn't had that. Their families might have been looking for them, but they wouldn't know where to start. Davey had.

And clearly, so had Franklin. Evan had questions, and he wanted answers. "How did you know they were in a lab?" he asked.

Franklin eyed him. "Is this a test?"

"Consider it one. If you fail it, my roots might not take it well."

Franklin looked scared, which wasn't something Evan was used to. People weren't scared of him. They found him cute and sometimes adorable, but not scary. Even when he'd threatened some of the doctors and the guards, no one had been scared of him.

Until Franklin.

Evan wiggled his fingers. Maybe he didn't hate this new ability, after all. He'd have to learn to live with it. He might as well enjoy it, right?

"Maybe stop trying to scare him," Hansen murmured.

Evan was relieved that his mate hadn't gone far. As soon as he was done getting answers out of Franklin, he'd dragged Hansen home and *not* to get clothes. No, he had every intention of getting Hansen *out* of the clothing he was wearing. Hansen looked good in a doctor's white coat, but he'd look even better naked, especially if Evan was allowed to add a bonding mark to his neck.

"I'm not going to hurt you," he told Franklin, even though he wasn't sure he'd be able to control it.

Franklin didn't look convinced, but he nodded anyway. "It took me a long time. At first, I focused on my mother. She survived long enough to tell me that someone had taken my siblings, but she couldn't give me any details. I went back to the scene where the car had crashed and got my hands on the incident report. It snowballed from there. I found out about the labs through the hunters."

"The hunters caused the crash," Hansen said.

It wasn't a question. They all knew that was how hunters operated.

"They did. I followed them and attempted to infiltrate their ranks, but it was impossible. I still wanted to find Leah and

Garrett, though, so I did the next best thing and focused on the labs. I've been working in as many labs as I could find since I started this."

And he still hadn't found his siblings. Evan's heart bled for this man. He wished he could do more, but at the same time, there was nothing anyone could do. Leah and Garrett were lost in the labs. The only way for Franklin to find them was to be incredibly lucky, and so far, he hadn't been.

*

Hansen was relieved when Evan's roots let go of Franklin. He didn't know the guy, but from the little he'd seen of him, he didn't deserve to get skewered by a root, especially by accident. Hansen doubted that Evan had a good grasp of his ability yet—he hadn't even known he had it when Hansen had left for the raid a few hours ago.

Hansen knew how nervous and anxious Evan had been about having an ability that could potentially hurt people, so he was glad that it wasn't anything as dramatic as Teddy's ability to explode things—and people. Evan would have to work on his control and his emotions, but Hansen knew he could do it. He wasn't worried.

178

Much.

"Thank you, Evan," Rikar said.

Hansen blinked at him. He'd been so focused on making sure that Evan didn't do something he shouldn't that he hadn't seen the leader coming closer. Rikar had taken control of the scene when Hansen and the others had arrived, and the wounded were already being taken to the healers, so Hansen wouldn't have to worry about them. He only had to worry about Evan and finding some clothes to cover himself. He really needed to remember not to shift on raids.

Evan grimaced. "Yeah, sorry about this and what happened earlier."

"You have nothing to apologize for."

"I wrapped you up in roots."

"You were emotional and had never used your ability before. I don't hold it against you, and I don't think you should hold it against yourself, either. Now, why don't you take Hansen home? As much as I appreciate the sight of a nice pair of legs, he should probably get dressed. I don't know how many people Moore is bringing back, but we might need his help."

"When do you need us back?"

There was something in Evan's expression that told Hansen that he was planning something. Hansen wasn't sure what it was, but he was slightly worried. Evan was settling into his new life, and it showed. He was more open with people and didn't hesitate to do or say things as much as he had before, and Hansen felt humbled that he was allowed to see it and to be part of Evan's life. Still, the way Evan kept glancing at him was slightly worrying, especially when Evan took Hansen's hand and dragged him away.

Hansen heard Matthew laugh, so he flipped him the bird without looking back. Matthew laughed harder, but Hansen was focused on Evan, who clearly had something on his mind. He didn't let anything or anyone stop him as they made their way to Hansen's house, and he didn't hesitate to push open the door when they reached it.

Evan had been staying with Hansen more often than not these days. It was good for their relationship and for the one between Davey and Orion, and Hansen hoped it would soon become a permanent move.

"Okay," Evan said as he stopped in the middle of the small entrance and turned to face Hansen. "I thought we'd have more time, but Rikar made it sound like Moore will expect you to be there when he comes back, so we'll have to be quick."

He whipped off his t-shirt, and Hansen stared.

It was far from the first time he saw Evan without his shirt on—or without anything on. As always, his cock reacted to the sight, even though he still had no idea what Evan was talking about. He stood there, half-naked, and Hansen's brain had short-circuited.

"Hansen?"

Hansen cleared his throat to give himself a moment. "I'm not sure what you're asking for."

"We need to bond."

That wasn't what Hansen had expected, although, to be fair, he hadn't actually known what he should expect. "What?" he croaked.

"I'm not going through this again. I—I didn't know what was happening to you. I realize that even if I had, I wouldn't have been able to do anything about it, but at least I would've known, and you would've been able to feel me, too. I need that, Hansen. I'm not letting you out of my sight again until we're bonded. I can't."

Hansen understood where Evan was coming from. He also

didn't think they were rushing. They were pretty much living together, and fulfilling the bond between them would only solidify their relationship. He wanted it as much as Evan did, and he didn't even care that Evan wanted to bond so he could be sure that Hansen would be okay.

He never seemed to be able to say no to his mate, and this request wasn't any different. "Okay."

Evan stared at him for a moment. "Yeah?"

"Yeah. You want to bond, and I'm okay with that."

"Are you okay with it, or do you want the same? Because I won't force you into something you're not ready for."

Hansen smiled. He didn't believe that Evan would force him into anything, even though it had sounded like he might earlier. Evan knew what he wanted, and what he wanted was to bond with Hansen.

"I'm sure, although I probably should shower first."

Evan smiled slowly. "Or we could shower together, you know, to avoid wasting water."

Hansen laughed and pulled Evan into his arms. "Wasting water?"

"I'm thinking of the environment."

Hansen doubted that Evan was actually thinking of the

environment with this suggestion, but it didn't matter. He was fine showering with his mate. In fact, he'd be more than happy to do so. "Let's go shower."

He didn't have to say it twice. Evan stepped away from him and grabbed his hand, then dragged him toward the stairs. Hansen laughed again. He was happy, so much so that sometimes, it was hard to believe. This was what he'd wanted when he'd been desperate to meet his mate. He hadn't known it would be Evan, but he'd known they would make each other happy, and he hoped that he and Evan would have the opportunity to do so for years to come.

Evan almost fell on his face as he rushed up the stairs. He was excited, and Hansen was happy to see it. They weren't only bonding because Evan needed reassurance when Hansen was working. They were doing it because Evan wanted it. They both did.

"Why a lab coat?" Evan asked as they walked into the bathroom off the bedroom they shared.

"It was the easiest thing to take off one of the docs and put on. I wouldn't have been comfortable leaving someone naked because I needed pants." Hansen stuck a leg forward. "Why? You don't like it?"

"I love it, although I wish people would stop staring at your legs. Rikar wasn't lying when he said they were nice."

"And they're all yours."

Evan raised his chin. "Damn right, they are." He reached for the lab coat and started unbuttoning it. Hansen batted his hands away and took over since that was all he was wearing, while Evan still had to get rid of the rest of his clothes.

As soon as Hansen was naked, he turned on the water. He dragged Evan into the shower, but when Evan pressed against him, he pushed him away. "Let me clean up. I don't want to bond with you while stinking of sweat."

Evan groaned. "I don't care what you smell like. I just want your fangs in my neck."

A shiver ran up Hansen's back. "I wish we had more time."

"Do you think Moore's going to look for you if you're not there when he arrives?"

"Probably. With the number of hunters present at the lab, Moore's going to need all-hands-on-deck."

Evan reached for the soap. "Fine. Let's get this party on the road."

Maybe Hansen should care that this wasn't a romantic moment filled with candles and roses. He didn't. At the end of the day, the result would be the same — he and Evan would be bonded.

That was why he didn't hesitate when Evan tilted his head sideways after washing him up as quickly as he could. He buried his face against Evan's neck and inhaled his mate's scent.

He'd always thought it was cliché, but it really felt like coming home. Something in him settled, and he knew that no matter what happened in the future, he would always have this. Evan would always be by his side, to support him and comfort him, to help him whenever he needed help, to hold him when he was sad, and he would do the same for Evan.

A jolt of pain pulled him out of his thoughts. Clearly, Evan was losing his patience because he'd just bitten Hansen. He wasn't wrong. They didn't have much time, which meant that Hansen needed to get to work, too.

He sank his fangs into Evan's neck. Evan whimpered and pressed close, and Hansen wasn't surprised to feel that he was hard. He cupped his hands around Evan's ass and hauled him up. Evan never leaned back from Hansen's neck. He continued sucking at the wound he'd created even as Hansen pressed him against the shower wall.

Evan's blood slid smoothly down Hansen's throat as they rutted against each other. Evan clung to Hansen as if he never wanted to let him go, and Hansen hoped he wouldn't. He needed his mate to never let go.

Hansen heard a phone ringing in the distance, but he didn't pay it much attention. He could feel the bond between him and Evan linking them fully together. He could feel Evan's pleasure and the love he felt for Hansen.

They came at the same time when their bond snapped into place. The sensations were too much, and Hansen pressed Evan harder against the wall, shuddering against him as the warm water hit his shoulders. They were both panting, but Hansen was in heaven. The bond was there, telling him that Evan was tired but happy.

The phone started ringing again. Evan groaned and slumped against Hansen. "I think that means that Moore's looking for you."

"Unfortunately, I think you're right." Hansen carefully let Evan back to his feet. "But it won't be forever. We'll be done in a few hours."

Evan grinned. "I'll be waiting for you here at home when you are."

Home. That was what Evan had said, even though they hadn't talked about this being his home. That was fine. They didn't need to talk about it. Evan *was* home.

CHAPTER SEVEN

Evan narrowed his eyes when Olga and her mate came in. He glanced back at Moore and Jolyn, who were sitting at a table with Rikar and Hayes. What was happening? Why were they all here? Had something happened that Evan didn't know about?

The back door was open, so Evan leaned in. Orion was showing Davey how to spread the cookie dough, while Hansen was eating a cupcake in a corner. His eyes widened when he saw that Evan had noticed him, and he stuffed the rest of the cupcake into his mouth.

Evan rolled his eyes. "What is it with you and cupcakes?"

Orion glanced in Hansen's direction. "Leave my cupcakes alone."

"It was one," Hansen argued. "It's nothing like what happened last time. I'm sorry I had to sell your cupcakes to save Evan from a horde of hungry children, but you got fifty dollars out of it. *I* should be the one selling your stuff, really."

"Are you trying to steal my job?" Evan asked.

"I wouldn't dream of it."

Evan believed it. Hansen loved what he did too much to want another job, and even if he did, he would never take it away from Evan. This wasn't why Evan was here, though. "Do you know if Moore called for a meeting?" he asked Orion.

Orion frowned. "What do you mean? What meeting?"

"They're all in the front room."

Davey and Hansen exchanged a glance and moved almost as one. They didn't look like they knew about it, but if there was anything to find out, they would. After Evan let them pass, he followed them.

The bakery was quiet except for their friends. Luckily, the morning rush had come and gone, and the lunch rush hadn't come yet, so there weren't many customers. Evan quickly took care of the two women waiting at the counter while he kept an eye on Hansen's people.

"Has something happened?" Davey asked when the women left.

Moore frowned at him, then looked around the room and shook his head. "I know what it looks like, but it's a coincidence."

"I'm only here for the cookies," Hayes added as he picked up his and took a bite. He moaned, causing Moore to arch a brow at him.

Evan pushed past Davey and flopped onto the chair in front of Moore. "You looked into Franklin?"

Moore smiled, visibly amused. "I just said this wasn't a meeting."

"It's not. It's me asking about Franklin." Evan wanted to be sure that Franklin was telling the truth before he felt pity for him.

Everything Franklin had said about his siblings had sounded true, but how was Evan supposed to know? He couldn't, which was why he'd asked Moore to look into it. If Franklin had told the truth, Moore would find out. Hell, if he really had siblings who'd been kidnapped by the hunters,

Moore and the mutants would help him find them.

It wouldn't be easy or fast. Nothing was when the hunters and the labs were involved. The doctors and whoever was funding the operation were smart and sneaky, and they knew what they were doing. They knew how to hide the labs and the people they kidnapped.

But escaping the labs was possible. Evan wouldn't be here today if it wasn't.

"I did look into him," Moore confirmed. "As far as I could find, everything he said is true. I found reports of the accident and newspaper articles about it and the death of his mother. His siblings haven't been seen since then. He filed missing person reports, but no one has been able to find them."

"Something needs to be done about the labs," Hayes murmured as he picked at what was left of his cookie. "We're rescuing as many people as we can, but there are so many more still trapped. We need to get to the head of this because taking the labs down one by one isn't working."

"How?" Hansen asked. He wrapped an arm around Evan's shoulders and squeezed him close.

"I don't know about the labs, but it would be near impossible to do that for the hunters," Orion interjected.

191

"They don't have a leader or anything like that. The hunters live in small groups, more often families. You can take out some of them, but there will always be more."

"I feel like the labs and the hunters are two separate things. We might not be able to completely get rid of the hunters, but if we do manage to close all the labs, they won't have anyone to sell people to. They might stop kidnapping so many people if they can't do anything with them."

"So our main goal should be the labs."

"I agree," Moore declared. "The problem is that we don't know who's at the head of the operation. They've been careful. We haven't found anything in the documents we managed to get our hands on in any of the labs we raided."

"Maybe it's time to bring in the council," Jolyn suggested. He patted his mate's hand. "I know you don't trust them, but it's clear that you and mutants can't do this on your own. Hayes is right. You can continue raiding labs, but as long as you don't know who's funding them, there will always be more labs and more people getting hurt."

Evan didn't know the history between Moore and the council, but he was curious. The council was supposed to protect shifters and supernatural creatures, so he found it strange that they weren't helping Moore and his mutants. He'd asked Hansen about it, but Hansen had just grimaced and had tried to distract Evan. It had, mostly because they'd been alone, and Hansen had lured Evan into bed, but he couldn't do that now.

"What's wrong with the council?" Evan asked.

Moore groaned. "I don't like them."

"And?"

"That's it, really. They failed us. The council might have been created to protect us, but over the years, it's become more about keeping humans happy than doing that. If they were truly working to protect us, they would've found a way to stop the labs. I'm not even sure they know the labs exist. They probably thought that after the Glass Research Company was closed, they would never have to deal with anything like this again. It's easier for them to ignore all of this and leave it in our hands."

"But my family will help you if you ask them," Jolyn said. "They work for the council, but you're more important."

"Fine," Moore said with a smile. "We can contact your brother and see what he thinks of this. I don't want the council involved, but I can deal with a bunch of assassins."

Evan blinked. "I'm sorry?"

Hansen's arm tightened around him, and he leaned closer. "I'll tell you later," he whispered.

Evan wasn't sure he could wait that long. "Assassins?" he whispered back.

Hansen glanced at the group, but they were talking about ways to find who was funding the labs. They probably wouldn't hear Hansen explain. Evan didn't care if they did. He wanted to know, dammit.

"Jolyn and his twin brother are healers for a bunch of council-trained assassins. Jolyn lives in the village now, but he still works with them when they need him."

"What do you mean, assassins?"

"Exactly what I said. The council trained them to take out the people they wanted taken out. They're very good at what they do."

"Why aren't they going on raids instead of you, then?"

"They help sometimes, but their job is specific. When the council needs them to kill someone, they do it. They don't work for Moore or the mutants. They work for the council."

"Jolyn just said they were family."

"Which is why they'll probably help."

Evan understood why going on raids and helping people was so important to his mate, which was why he hadn't tried to get Hansen to stop. If the council and their assassins finally stepped in to help, there would be even fewer possibilities of Hansen getting hurt. Eventually, he might not even have to go on raids.

Evan didn't know these people, and he was a little scared of them, but he already loved them.

The mutants needed help. They needed to stop the person funding the labs, close all of them, and, once that was done, move on to the hunters. They wouldn't be as dangerous as they were now once the labs were closed, but they couldn't be allowed to continue hurting people.

It seemed like they had a game plan, and Evan hoped it would work. He needed it to.

He needed to finally be allowed to leave the labs behind so he could focus on his future with Hansen.

ABOUT THE AUTHOR

Catherine is the creator of several series, most of them paranormal, including the Whitedell Pride Series and the Gillham Pack Series. While she graduated in translation, she decided to go the writer's way because it was more fun to create her own stories and characters.

She lived in Italy for twenty-six years but has now returned home to the north of Europe.

She loves pizza—probably too much—her son, her pets, and of course, books. She sneaks some reading time into her schedule every time she has five minutes free from writing, demands from her various pets, and son, and lastly, housework.

www.ingramcontent.com/pod-product-compliance
Lightning Source LLC
Chambersburg PA
CBHW072109170626
46813CB00004B/1493